She smiled up at him with relief, with gratitude, and his heart gave a sharp tug in his chest.

He'd known that what had been done to her was diabolical. He'd never imagined just how incredibly cruel it had been. It verged on evil.

Then Claire's eyes widened slightly, as though just noticing how close he was. In that instant, something changed between them, a noticeable thickening of the air. Josh felt her closeness that keenly, even as part of him recognized she wasn't nearly close enough.

All it took was a glimpse of her sweet, soft mouth to send a charge through him.

How could any man resist?

KERRY CONNOR

BEAUTIFUL STRANGER

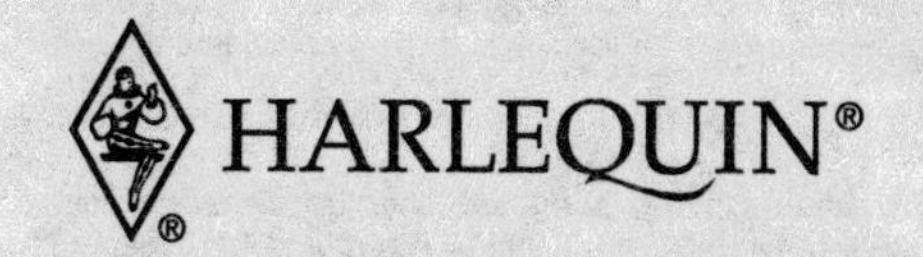

TORONTO • NEW YORK • LONDON
AMSTERDAM • PARIS • SYDNEY • HAMBURG
STOCKHOLM • ATHENS • TOKYO • MILAN • MADRID
PRAGUE • WARSAW • BUDAPEST • AUCKLAND

To my grandmother, for all the Intrigues.

ISBN-13: 978-0-373-69361-0
ISBN-10: 0-373-69361-3

BEAUTIFUL STRANGER

This edition published by arrangement with Harlequin Books S.A.

www.eHarlequin.com

Printed in U.S.A.

ABOUT THE AUTHOR

A lifelong mystery reader, Kerry Connor first discovered romantic suspense by reading Harlequin Intrigue books and is thrilled to be writing for the line. Kerry lives and writes in Southern California.

Books by Kerry Connor

HARLEQUIN INTRIGUE

1067—STRANGERS IN THE NIGHT
1094—BEAUTIFUL STRANGER

CAST OF CHARACTERS

Claire Preston—Locked away in a mental institution with no idea how or why she'd come to be there, she had no choice but to escape to get some answers.

Josh Bennett—The doctor couldn't turn away a woman in need of his help.

Milton Vaughn—The family attorney is in charge of Claire's inheritance until she turns thirty-five, and may not be willing to turn over control easily.

Gerald Preston—The uncle who felt he should rightfully control the family business.

Dinah Preston—Gerald's wife had always suspected Claire would cause the family embarrassment.

Thad Preston—Claire's cousin cared more about spending money than earning it.

Dr. Walter Emmons—The head of the Shady Point mental health facility had his price.

Karen Tate—Claire considered her assistant her friend. Had she made a mistake?

Ahmed Al-Saeed—Finding Claire was his mission, and nothing would stop him from fulfilling it.

Chapter One

Today was the day. She was finally going to escape this hellhole.

A heady mixture of adrenaline and fear rushed through her veins. Adrenaline because the day was finally here after three long months of waiting and planning. Fear because she knew this was her only chance. If she failed, she would be trapped here forever. Her life would effectively be over.

The thought sent another blast of anxiety through her, but Claire Preston allowed her body to betray none of her turbulent emotions. The breathing exercises and years of yoga she'd practiced helped her keep her heartbeat steady. Her eyes remained fixed on an empty space on the lawn in front of her. She didn't move a muscle, other than a slight bob of her head to relieve the growing crick in her neck. Even that could easily be viewed as an unconscious twitch by anyone who might be looking. There was absolutely nothing that might lead anyone to think she was anything more than what she appeared to be.

Just another patient at the Thornwood mental health facility, so drugged out of her mind she didn't even know who she was anymore.

Except Claire did know. Just as she knew the only way that would continue to be the case was if no one else was aware of that fact.

Voices drifted toward her as people passed by on the edges of the lawn, none of them paying her any mind. Late afternoon sunlight poured down over the veranda where one of the nurses had parked and abandoned her. Claire felt none of its warmth. She'd felt nothing but a bone-chilling cold from the moment she'd woken up in this place and found herself living her worst nightmare.

More than once she'd wondered if this was really happening or if it was all in her head. She didn't know what would be worse, being sane and locked up in a mental institution, or figuring out this was a hallucination and she really was crazy after all.

It hadn't taken her long to determine this was all too real. Nightmares didn't last this long.

But no more. It was time for this nightmare to end.

The voices finally faded from earshot. She waited and listened closely for the sound of anyone else approaching. Hearing nothing, she lifted her head slightly and scanned the area.

The lawn stretched before her, lush and green, seeming to go on forever. She had to fight the urge to bolt, to lunge out of the chair and make a break for it as fast as her legs could carry her.

Not yet. But soon.

A flicker of movement in the corner of her vision drew her eye. It was a man, walking toward her on the path bordering the lawn. The sunshine at his back, he seemed to rise out of the horizon. Dismissing him, she quickly looked away, only to find her attention drawn back for some reason a moment later.

More details became visible the closer he came. He was a stranger. She recognized that much. She'd never seen him before.

The sunlight caught his dark blond hair, burnishing it with a golden glow. He had the big, brawny body of an athlete, with broad shoulders and biceps that filled the contours of the dark suit he wore. His long, confident stride, not quite a swagger, but close, told of a man at complete ease with himself. It was the kind of effortless confidence she'd always envied, even resented maybe. Even from a distance, she could see the slight smile on his face. He had a nice face. Friendly. Open. Incredibly good-looking.

He moved like some kind of conquering hero, every inch the hale, hearty knight in complete command of himself and his world. No one would ever accuse this man of being insane.

He looked like someone who could help her. Someone she could trust.

She didn't know where the thought came from. Something painful twisted in her chest at the very idea. She couldn't remember the last time she'd thought that about another human being, if ever.

She tried to dismiss it. Instead, a burst of longing seized her, so fierce and unexpected she lost control of her heartbeat for a moment. For just a second, she allowed herself the foolish fantasy that the knight had come to save the princess trapped in a tower, before forcing herself to face cold, hard reality.

No white knight was going to step out of a fairy tale and save her.

No one ever had and no one ever would.

This princess was going to have to save herself.

SOMEONE WAS WATCHING HIM.

Josh Bennett was halfway to the building when the unmistakable feeling swept over him. The main building of the Thornwood psychiatric hospital featured a multitude of windows overlooking the back lawn. He scanned them with a quick glance, but didn't see anyone looking out at him.

Still, the feeling persisted. A whisper of unease slid down his spine.

Trying to shake it off, he continued toward the building.

Then he saw her.

She was sitting on the deck overlooking the lawn. The robe she was wearing left little doubt that she was a patient. She must be the one who was watching him.

The explanation came as something of a relief. He'd felt uneasy ever since he'd arrived at Thornwood. Then again, many people probably were when it came to mental hospitals, regardless of their own sanity, especially one as imposing as this one. The century-old building was massive and grim, sprawling atop a small hill like some kind of crouching beast. Even in broad daylight on a bright, cloudless afternoon, an air of gloom hung over it.

He'd never considered himself easily spooked, but this place was enough to get to him. As a result, he'd likely been placing more importance on his previously unseen watcher than was necessary. He had to smile at his own foolishness.

As he walked closer, Josh couldn't help but notice that the woman was almost absurdly beautiful. He might have believed she was a statue carved by a great artist. Her face was that flawless. High cheekbones. A straight little nose. A ripe, full mouth. Dark brown hair brushed the tops of her shoulders, a few flyaway strands fluttering in the breeze.

Yet there was an aura of sadness around her as she sat there, alone and seemingly abandoned on the veranda. He wondered why she was here, what she was being treated for.

It was only when he'd almost reached the building that he saw what he'd been unable to from the distance. There was no expression on that beautiful face. Her eyes stared blankly in front of her.

Sympathy twisted his gut. She appeared completely unaware of her surroundings, lost in a world of her own. Evidently she hadn't been staring at him after all.

He was about to look away when her eyes suddenly shifted and caught his.

A jolt of awareness surged through him, as though a charge of pure electricity had passed between them through their locked gazes. Her eyes widened slightly, seeming surprised to have made contact with his. And for one heart-stopping moment, he saw something burning in her fevered gaze, a raw emotion he knew too well.

Fear.

No. More like pure terror.

Then, just as suddenly as they'd met his, her eyes seemed to lose focus and slowly rolled away.

The moment couldn't have lasted more than a few seconds, a brief enough time that he almost had to wonder if he'd imagined the whole thing. The pounding of his heart and the tension strumming through him told him he hadn't. No imaginary moment could have caused such a visceral reaction.

He stood frozen, waiting to see what she would do next,

wondering if he should go over and try to talk to her. If she needed help, there might be something he could do.

As he watched, her lips parted slightly.

He held his breath.

A bead of saliva slid out of the corner of her mouth and down her chin. She made no move to wipe it away.

He exhaled sharply. The woman clearly wasn't conscious of her surroundings. He must have imagined whatever he'd thought he'd seen in her eyes.

Still, he couldn't leave her sitting there with drool on her face. There didn't appear to be any nurses or orderlies around. He could at least do that for her.

He took a step toward her.

"Bennett! You made it!"

Josh looked up to see Dr. Aaron Harris striding through the doors of the facility toward him. Josh eased his expression into a practiced smile. "Barely. For a while there I wasn't sure they were going to let me onto the grounds."

Aaron matched his grin and extended his hand. "Let me guess. You're still driving that beat-up old wreck. How much duct tape does it take to hold that thing together these days?"

"Three rolls just about covers it," he quipped. He wondered idly what Aaron would think if he knew what Josh really drove most of the time. The other man probably wouldn't even believe it.

Aaron shook his head. "That's why we have to get you out of that city hospital. You're never going to make any real money working in the E.R."

"Believe it or not, some people actually think there are more important things in life than getting rich and spending money."

He might have imagined it, but for a second it seemed like the warmth in Aaron's smile cooled slightly. "Same old Josh. Still trying to save the world, huh? Did that trouble in the E.R. have anything to do with that?"

Josh gritted his teeth, but kept his smile intact. The story of an E.R. doc slugging a patient's husband in front of her had gotten enough play in the media that there probably wasn't a single person in the Philadelphia area who hadn't heard about it, especially when the husband in question had run crying to a lawyer.

The usual fury coiled in the pit of his stomach at the thought of that bastard. The man should be in jail, but Josh was the one facing a mess of trouble, on a forced leave of absence while the hospital decided what to do with him.

Rather than say any of that, he simply shrugged. "Oh, you know how it goes. Stressful environment, emotions running high. Things like that are bound to happen every once in a while."

"Happily, I don't. Dr. Emmons has done such a terrific job creating a peaceful environment for the patients here that it's a great working environment for the staff as well. Beats the E.R. hands down."

Dr. Walter Emmons, Josh knew from his research in preparation for this meeting, was the highly respected psychiatrist who ran Thornwood. "I have to admit, I was surprised when you called. We both know I'm not a psychiatrist."

"Of course. But most of our patients are long-term residents who require care beyond their mental needs. With your experiences in emergency medicine, I doubt there's too much we could throw at you that would surprise you. I think you'd be a valued member of our team." Aaron shook his head. "Listen to me ramble on. Come on. Let me show you around."

Josh felt the strain of keeping his smile in place, but Aaron didn't seem to notice. No one ever did. With a polite nod, he followed him into the building.

As they walked, Aaron launched into a recitation of the wonders of Thornwood. Josh listened with half an ear. He already knew he had no intention of taking the job. He'd only come at Beth's urging. She'd told him he was in no position to turn down any job offers out of hand when he might be in need of a new one fairly soon. Faced with that logic, he hadn't been able to say no.

The job certainly seemed to suit Aaron. Josh hadn't seen his old classmate since back in med school, but it didn't look like he'd changed much. Still effortlessly smooth, still dressed to the nines. Josh wouldn't be surprised if Aaron's shirt had cost more than his entire outfit. Aaron had always been a little too slick for Josh's tastes, but it seemed to work for him. Back in school, they'd been on friendly terms, but never particularly close. The last he'd heard about him were rumblings of some sort of trouble he'd gotten into at the hospital in Chicago where he'd done his residency. Busy with his own life, Josh hadn't paid much attention at the time. Whatever the trouble might have been, it seemed like Aaron had landed on his feet.

And now he was the one with a job opportunity for an old classmate in trouble of his own. But Josh wasn't looking for a cushy job where he could get paid well for doing little. He could tell he'd be bored out of his mind working somewhere like this.

Not to mention the place gave him the creeps.

The uneasy feeling had only increased when they'd stepped inside. An unsettling sensation slid across his skin. He suppressed a shudder.

He couldn't quite explain the feeling, especially when the inside was less forbidding than the exterior. Though the building obviously showed its age, the facilities appeared well maintained. The first floor featured high ceilings and all those windows that let in the sunlight and made the space feel open and airy. The tiled floors beneath their feet gleamed. The formerly state-run hospital had been taken over by a private corporation a decade earlier, with the state now paying it to house patients who had nowhere else to go. From all appearances, the company that now owned Thornwood was doing a bang-up job, as well as pulling in a decent enough profit that they could still pay Aaron a better salary than a city hospital could.

But despite the tranquil surface, the atmosphere was charged with something else. Bad vibes, Josh thought. For one thing, it was eerily quiet—not in a peaceful way, but a distinctly unnatural one. Odd for a hospital. Other than Aaron prattling on beside him, the building resounded with silence.

They passed a television lounge where several patients stared glassily, only a few at the actual TV, its volume set to a barely intelligible murmur. Each of them appeared as lost in their own minds as the woman he'd seen on his way in.

The woman.

The thought of her brought the terrified look in her eyes back to him. Aaron had appeared and pulled him away before he'd had a chance to try to speak to her. Now he wished he'd had just a few seconds to do so, to confirm for himself at least that everything was all right with her.

He glanced back just before they turned a corner.

It was too late. She was already out of view.

"OKAY. THAT'S ENOUGH SUN for one day."

It took every ounce of willpower Claire possessed not to jump at the sound of that low, cruel voice in her ear. It helped that she'd known it was coming. She didn't have to see Jerry Hobbs to know he was nearby. She'd become so attuned to the orderly's presence her skin always began to crawl whenever he was around.

This time, though, his presence was a good thing. She'd been waiting impatiently all afternoon, not to mention the three months prior.

The time was finally here. Her pulse might have jumped if she didn't have it firmly under control.

As usual, he leaned too close, the scent of cheap, sickeningly sweet cologne washing over her, and murmured directly in her ear. Her immediate instinct was to lean away from him. She managed not to.

This is it. This is the last time.

A few seconds later, he wheeled her off the veranda toward her room.

None of the staff she'd encountered at Thornwood had much of a bedside manner, but Hobbs was the worst. He hauled her in and out of bed and the wheelchair as carelessly as he would handle a laundry bag. The bruises on her arms and torso were proof enough of that.

If the injuries he'd inflicted had been solely the result of carelessness, it would have been bad enough. But Claire suspected that wasn't the case. One time when he'd grabbed her wrist, she'd sensed him watching her face as he'd slowly squeezed with greater and greater force. She'd wondered if he was testing her, trying to see if she would reveal her deception if he hurt her. She hadn't, somehow managing to keep from reacting to the pain. Only when he'd left had she cradled her aching wrist to her side and let out the whimper of agony she'd managed to swallow. A brief moment, but a telling one. He liked inflicting pain. And at least one instance when the back of his hand had rubbed against her breast had lingered too long to be an accident.

The nurses must have noticed her injuries, but Hobbs was still around. She suspected no one had reported him. Maybe they were looking out for each other. Maybe they were afraid of him. Maybe they just didn't care.

As they made their way to her room on the second floor, she carefully glanced at her surroundings to get a sense of how many people were around. The halls were mostly deserted, something that would only help her.

Finally they arrived at her room. Hobbs wheeled her inside, closing the door behind them with a noticeable click.

Keeping her body utterly still, Claire tensed inwardly, ready for her moment.

For months she'd had no choice but to sit there and take it, knowing she couldn't break the charade.

Not today.

Never again.

He stopped in front of the chair and reached for her.

Before he had a chance to wrap his slimy fingers around her arm, she reached up and caught his wrist in midair.

His shocked eyes met hers.

She didn't say a word. Her other hand was already arcing toward his face.

The heel of her hand made direct contact with his nose. She felt the bone break with a satisfying crunch. Almost simultaneously, her foot kicked out and caught him in the crotch before he had a chance to scream. Releasing his wrist as he doubled over, she lashed out again, sending her fist straight into his stomach. One last punch crashed into his jaw.

He crumpled into a heap, his head smacking against the floor with a thud.

Just to make sure he was unconscious, she nudged him with her foot.

His chest rose and fell, but otherwise he didn't move.

Triumph swelled within her. It had taken a while before she could use them, but those self-defense classes had come in handy after all.

She shot a nervous glance back at the door to see if anyone had noticed through the window what had happened. The attack couldn't have lasted more than five seconds. Had anyone seen?

There was nobody at the window, no sounds of an alarm being raised in the corridor.

Taking that as a sign she was in the clear, she wasted no time lunging from the chair. For a second her head swam and her legs wobbled beneath her. She spent only a few precious seconds waiting for them to steady, then started moving again, reaching for Hobbs. Hopefully if she kept moving, her momentum would keep her on her feet. She was going to need all the help she could get. It was already painfully clear her body wasn't responding as quickly or strongly as it had before she wound up here.

Grabbing Hobbs under his arms, she dragged him to the bed. Her muscles quivered under the strain. Luckily, he wasn't much taller than she was, so his limp form wasn't too hard to handle. When she got to the bed, she pushed the sheets back. Taking one deep breath, she girded her strength and heaved him onto the bed with every last bit of power she had. Somehow she managed to get him onto the mattress.

Unclipping his security badge from his belt, she turned his head toward the wall and pulled the sheets up over him. No one should check on her for at least another half an hour. If they didn't look too closely, this could buy her even more time, depending on how long it took Hobbs to wake up. What she wouldn't give for some of the drugs they'd been plying her with, just to be sure.

Darting for the door, Claire carefully checked the hall through the window. It was still quiet, with no one in sight. She slowly eased the door open, and with one last check, slipped out into the corridor.

There was a stairway five doors down from her room. Claire quickly made her way to it, keeping her head turning and her eyes moving both in front of and behind her. There were no security cameras in this hallway, so at least she didn't have to worry about that. No one had appeared in either direction by the time she made it to the stairwell. She checked it, too, before entering. Neither seeing nor hearing anyone, she slipped inside.

She took the stairs two at a time. This was where things got dicey. She had never been on the first floor on this side of the building. She only had a vague idea of what was there, but it was enough to know it was where she wanted to be.

Not for the first time she wished she could make her escape at night. Except that she had no idea of the layout of the grounds or whether Thornwood was surrounded by any kind of security fence along the far perimeter. She'd tried to keep her strength up and her muscles primed by moving around in her room at night, long after lights-out, but she doubted she had the stamina for any kind of long-distance run, even if she could manage to get over a fence. Judging from the way her body was already responding just from knocking out Hobbs and hauling him onto the bed, she wouldn't last long on her feet.

Her best chance of getting off the grounds was to catch a ride, and during the day it was more likely a vehicle would be leaving. She knew from listening to the sounds outside her window that the loading dock was somewhere nearby. Every Monday for the last three months a truck had made a delivery around this time. If she could get down to the dock and sneak onto the departing truck before anyone noticed she was gone, she'd have a fast way out of here.

She just had to hope Hobbs hadn't waited too long to retrieve her. Every second she'd spent out on that veranda had seemed like an eternity. They'd only started taking her outside in the last few weeks. She didn't know why they bothered, but the change in the schedule had thrown off her plans enough she'd had to wait a few days longer than expected.

Reaching the first floor, she yanked the door open and shot a quick glance in either direction. Seeing no one, she burst out into the corridor, easing the door shut behind her. Her best guess was that the loading dock was to the right, so she headed in that direction, sending up a prayer that she'd chosen correctly.

She moved quickly but quietly, her slippered feet silent on the linoleum. The fluorescent lights flickered unsteadily, casting shadows on the sickly green walls. She swallowed her nervousness and kept moving.

After turning two more corners, Claire found herself facing a set of double doors at the end of another corridor.

The faint rumble of a large engine emanating from behind them was unmistakable.

Hurrying to them, she pressed her ear against the doors to try to detect any voices or footsteps inside. Hearing none, she waved Hobbs's pass in front of the security scanner. The lock released with an audible click. With painstaking slowness, she cracked the door open a fraction and peeked inside.

And watched with stunned horror as a truck, no doubt the one she'd been hoping to catch, pulled away from the dock.

There was no time to lament this turn of events. Staring into the open space, she quickly considered her options. Despite this setback, they hadn't changed much. She still needed to catch a ride out of here.

Maybe another truck would pull in immediately afterward to take the last one's place. Doubtful, but a possibility. Otherwise, she would need to find a car. Either way, cutting through the loading dock was the best and fastest way to get outside.

Silence hung in the large, empty space. The far end of the room was wide open, filling it with fading sunlight. Ninety feet and she'd be outdoors. Poking her head through the opening, she looked to see if anyone was around. It appeared deserted. She eased through the doorway and took one last look around the room from ceiling to floor, just to be certain. Still nothing.

As sure as she could be, she dashed across the room, moving on the balls of her feet to minimize the sound. At the end of the dock she raced down a few short steps to ground level, burst around the corner and threw her back against the wall. Relief barely penetrated. Now that she was outside, she felt even more exposed. She had to find cover.

There was a parking lot a short distance away, across the driveway and a short stretch of lawn to her left. The rows of cars gleamed in the sunlight, each offering a possible escape. The sight practically called to her.

She started in that direction, crouching down and staying near the building so no one looking out a window could see her. Within seconds she reached a spot that gave her a straight shot to the parking lot. She drew in a shuddery breath and checked in every direction.

And ran.

It couldn't have lasted more than thirty seconds, but the mad dash to the parking lot seemed like a thousand times longer. By the time she crashed to the pavement between two cars it felt like her heart had pounded through her chest.

Her breathing coming in short, rapid gasps, she slowly counted to ten, waiting for the sounds of running feet or raised voices, any sign that she'd been seen. None came. Even if someone had seen her and notified security, there wouldn't be any immediate sign for her to know. She had to keep moving. First and foremost, she needed to find a car that would get her out of here ASAP.

Rising to her haunches, she quickly poked her head up just enough to see through the window of the car she was hiding behind and looked around.

Then she saw him, a familiar figure appearing out of the horizon just as he had the first time, now heading toward the parking lot.

It was the man she'd seen before. Hobbs must have left her sitting on the veranda for an eternity if the newcomer had conducted his business and was just now leaving.

She felt a surge of excitement. Great timing. He would be the perfect person to catch a ride with. He wasn't a shrink and he didn't work here. Combined with the fact that he was leaving, that just about made him her favorite person in the world at the moment.

He was still far enough away that she should be able to get to his car long before he did. She remembered what the other doctor had said to him. He drove a beat-up old wreck.

It didn't take her long to spot the sedan. The back window bore a parking sticker from Center City General in downtown Philadelphia, no doubt the hospital where the other doctor said this one worked. The car had to be a couple of decades old, its paint faded and chipped. Not exactly a car she would have thought belonged to a doctor, but maybe he was paying off med-school bills, especially if he worked at a low-paying city hospital.

Unlike most of the cars in the lot, it was unlikely this one was equipped with any kind of alarm. Heck, its owner probably wouldn't even feel the need to lock it.

For the first time in four long months her lips curved into a smile.

Maybe the knight could come to her rescue after all.

And the best part was, he didn't even have to know.

Chapter Two

He'd sold his soul to the devil.

Dr. Walter Emmons had suspected as much for some time now, ever since the day he'd admitted Claire Preston to Thornwood for a considerable fee above the norm.

Staring into the dead eyes of the man standing before him erased what little doubt remained in his mind.

"How long has she been gone?" his visitor demanded.

"At least an hour. That's when the orderly took her back to her room. He was found about fifteen minutes later, and I was immediately notified." And when the first search produced no results, he'd made the decision to contact the man who'd paid him to keep her here, figuring it would be far worse to have him learn about her disappearance some other way, like having her turn up on his doorstep without warning.

Thirty minutes later, despite his assurances that the situation was under control, this man had arrived at Thornwood at the other's behest. And Walter Emmons wished he'd kept his mouth shut.

The man was tall, well over six feet, and lean, with dark olive skin and black hair cut close to the scalp. But it was the eyes Emmons couldn't look away from, no matter how much he wanted to. They seemed to be all pupil, two glowing black orbs that focused unerringly on his face and seemed to burn right through him. He didn't think the man had blinked once since he'd arrived.

His clinical side kicked in, and he knew without a doubt this man should be a patient in a facility like this, not responsible for tracking one down.

"How did this happen?" the man, who hadn't introduced himself other than to say who'd sent him, demanded.

"I don't know. I've been monitoring her medication closely—" a lie "—and every indication was that she was in a catatonic state." Every indication being the reports from his staff he'd relied on so foolishly. He'd been assured that Claire Preston was unaware of her surroundings, her mind broken. Clearly, she'd managed to fool them all.

"What are you doing about finding her?"

"I have people checking the grounds and the building in case she's still here. I've also had security review the surveillance tapes from the gate. Only three vehicles left the premises in the time span between when she was last seen and when her disappearance was discovered. We've already contacted two of the drivers, and neither has seen her. We're still trying to get in touch with the third driver. If she somehow managed to sneak out in a car, it must have been with him."

"Give me the address. I will go there."

Emmons blanched. "We don't know for sure that she escaped with the third driver. We're still trying to contact him."

"And in the meantime, she may be getting farther away. You said if she escaped it must have been with him. Were you wrong about that as well?"

"No, I—"

"Then give me the address." He practically spat the words.

Emmons swallowed hard. "At least let me send a team with you. This man is a doctor. He may be reluctant to send her off with anyone other than authorized Thornwood personnel."

The man appeared to consider this. After a brief pause, he signaled his agreement with a sharp nod of his head.

Emmons reached for the phone. "Even if she's not with the third driver, rest assured, we will find her."

A trace of scorn flashed across the man's face. "The same way you could be trusted to keep her here?"

"I made it clear from the beginning this is not a high-security facility."

"You also accepted money to ensure she would remain here. And you failed."

Emmons felt his face burn. Suddenly the mountain of gambling debts he was struggling to cover didn't seem like such a problem, only because it paled in comparison to the one literally staring him in the face at the moment.

He should have never let things get this far. He should have talked to a colleague about his addiction. He should have thought twice before digging himself into a hole of debt he had no hope of ever climbing out of.

He should have done a great many things. Except one.

"I never should have agreed to this," he muttered as he started dialing.

"But you did," the man said, his tone pitiless. "There is no turning back from it now."

No, there wasn't, Emmons thought. And now that this man had entered his life, he couldn't escape the terrifying feeling that his true problems were only just beginning.

THE THUMP WAS HIS first indication something was wrong.

After completing the long drive from Thornwood back home, Josh pulled into his garage, more than ready to change out of his suit and grab some food. He stepped on the brake. The car lurched to a stop.

And a definitive thump resounded from the trunk.

He froze, his weariness after the long day forgotten. An uneasy suspicion raised the hair at the back of his neck.

The trunk was supposed to be empty. The thump indicated it wasn't. Something was in there, something fairly sizeable from the sound of it.

Had someone put something in the trunk? He couldn't imagine why. An animal might have climbed in, except he didn't know how any creature would have managed it.

That left a person. He hadn't stepped away from the car when he'd stopped for gas on the way back. The only place where he could have picked up a stowaway was Thornwood.

Josh quickly considered his options. Sitting in the car wasn't one of them. It occurred to him that anything—or anyone—in the trunk could get into the car through the backseat, and vice versa, which was the only way anyone could have gained access to the trunk in the first place. He'd already sat there long enough to raise suspicions in the mind of any unwanted passenger that he was onto them.

He shifted the vehicle into park and shut off the engine, then hit the remote control to close the garage door before climbing out of the car. If there was someone in the trunk, particularly someone from Thornwood, he didn't want them to get away. He was in enough trouble without setting a mental patient loose.

Once outside the car, he flipped the switch next to the

kitchen door to keep the garage light on, not about to have it go out and leave him in the dark with whomever might be in there. He reached for the heavy wrench he'd left sitting next to the step after working on the leaky kitchen sink. The weight of it felt good in his hand. There was no telling if he'd need it, but he wasn't about to take any chances.

He moved to the back of the vehicle. Lifting the wrench above his head, he braced himself, then slid the key in the lock and threw the trunk open.

A pair of familiar brown eyes—wide and gaping with familiar terror—stared back at him.

He barely had time to react to his discovery when the woman lunged forward. Getting out of the trunk wasn't exactly the easiest proposition with her body practically curled into the fetal position. She somehow managed it, albeit without much grace, heaving herself out of the enclosed space and landing on the floor in front of him.

He took a step back out of her way, but didn't stop her. He hadn't wanted anybody in his trunk to begin with. He wasn't going to argue with her vacating it.

Once on her own two feet, she stood before him, her chest heaving, her body tense and fidgety. Her eyes darted every which way, clearly seeking an escape. He saw the moment she realized that, with the garage door closed, the only exits were the two doors in the near back corner of the garage—one leading outside, one into the house—and he was standing between her and the door.

Her eyes narrowed a fraction as her gaze shot up and down his body. Probably gauging her chances of rushing him and getting around him. From the way her lips thinned and she swallowed hard, she must have decided they weren't good.

"Calm down," he said in his most soothing tone, the one that had been known to settle down even the most terrified child in the E.R. "I'm not going to hurt you."

In response, her eyes flicked to the wrench he still held aloft.

He slowly lowered it to his side, keeping himself on alert to defend himself if necessary. Not that he would probably need the wrench for that. Viewing her in a standing position for the first time, he could see that she was no more than five-six at the most, and thin. He had more than half a foot and a hundred pounds on her, easy. But he knew nothing about this woman or why she'd been at Thornwood, or what she was capable of. After all, the last time he'd seen her, she'd seemed completely unaware of her surroundings, with drool running down her face.

Only that brief moment when their eyes met had indicated she was lucid—and scared. The fear was still there, along with a fierce determination, and this time there was no doubting she was fully cognizant. He suspected if he dropped the wrench, she'd be on him in a heartbeat, scratching and clawing and kneeing, in her desperation to get away. He would defend himself if he had to, but he really didn't want to hurt her.

He tried the soothing tone again. "Take it easy. Let's both take a breath and see if we can't talk for a second."

"There's nothing to talk about," she shot back. Her voice was hoarse as though from disuse, yet calm despite her obvious tension. "Look, you don't have to get involved. Just let me go and you can forget you even saw me."

"It's not that simple. I have to believe it's not going to take the folks back at Thornwood long to figure out that you're gone and, when they don't find you on the grounds, start contacting anyone who left at roughly the time you disappeared."

"All you have to do is tell them you don't know anything about me, and you're off the hook."

"I don't think I can do that."

A knowing gleam entered her straightforward gaze, and her mouth twisted with bitterness. "Because you don't want to be held responsible for letting a crazy person loose on the streets, right?"

"Are you crazy?" he said mildly.

He carefully watched her reaction. There was none of the anger or outrage he might have expected, merely what seemed like resignation. Interesting. "No." She lifted her hand against the skepticism she must have anticipated would greet the comment. "I know that's probably what all the mental patients say. But I'm not."

"All right," he said, privately reserving judgment. "I'm Josh, by the way. Josh Bennett. And you are?" he prodded when she said nothing.

She stared at him for a long moment, her eyes considering. He didn't know what she saw, but he suspected he hadn't been examined this thoroughly on his last credit check.

"Claire," she said finally.

She didn't elaborate further. He figured it wasn't worth pushing the point. "Okay, Claire. Why don't you tell me why you were at Thornwood?"

She sighed, the sound so full of weariness it tugged at something inside him. "I don't know. Four months ago I woke up there with no idea how I'd gotten there. This Dr. Emmons told me I'd suffered a mental breakdown. He didn't get into specifics, saying there was time for that later, and when I demanded answers, he just gave me this patronizing look, like I was a misbehaving child." She arched a brow, her expression turning wry. "Or a crazy person, I suppose. He just said they would take good care of me." She practically snorted at that. "The next thing I knew, they were sticking a needle in my arm and I was knocked out."

"What about the next time you saw him? Did he tell you more then?"

"I never saw him again. I was in and out of consciousness for the first month—out of it, mostly. Anytime anyone noticed that I was aware again, they'd bring out the needles. It didn't take me long to figure out if I didn't want to spend the rest of my life in a drug-induced haze, I couldn't let them know when the drugs wore off."

"So when I saw you sitting on the veranda this afternoon, you were pretending, with the drooling and all?"

She hesitated before answering, as if not sure how much to admit. "I have been for the past few months. Not all the time. They were still drugging me, of course, though I think they were lowering the dosage. Or maybe I was getting used to the drugs. Either way, I gradually started to be more aware. I just never let them see when I wasn't out of it anymore."

"And no one on staff noticed that you were pretending for, what, three months?"

In spite of his best efforts, he couldn't quite keep the disbelief out of his voice. It was clear she hadn't failed to notice.

"As long as I wasn't causing trouble, no one paid too much attention to me. I was never examined by a doctor while I was conscious, and it was obvious the nurses and orderlies were only there to cash a check. They did what was necessary to provide a basic level of care, but otherwise none of them gave me a second glance. I was basically invisible."

He couldn't help frowning. The image she painted wasn't the same Thornwood he'd heard wonderful things about, or the one he'd visited that afternoon. The place seemed a marvel of efficiency.

But that feeling he'd had when he was there, that something was somehow off about the place, nagged at him in a way that couldn't be attributed to a forbidding exterior. It wouldn't be the first case of something being too perfect to be believed, or at the very least, not all it seemed.

"Even so, you wouldn't have been admitted for no reason."

"But maybe for the right price."

"What are you saying? That they were paid to admit you?"

"And keep me there. Think about it. Why else would they fail to explain exactly why I'd been brought there? Why keep me drugged for months rather than offer any kind of therapy or professional treatment?"

"But who would do that? And why?"

She paused, her gaze sharpening. "Can I trust you to keep this conversation between the two of us?"

"You mean doctor/patient privilege? I'm not your doctor."

"Nor do I want you to be. I just want to know you won't repeat what I'm going to tell you."

He wondered who exactly she expected him to talk to, and why discretion was such an issue. Was she going to spin a story too easily proven false if he shared it with anyone else?

Still, he wanted to know what she was going to say. Confidentiality didn't seem too much to ask for, if he could help it. He just hoped she didn't force him to make a liar of himself. "All right."

She took a deep breath, as though gathering strength. "My name is Claire Preston. My family owns Preston Aeronautics and Defense. You may not have heard of it, but we're a private defense contractor that provides services to the government and the armed forces. It's a multi-billion-dollar corporation. Tomorrow is my thirty-fifth birthday. At that time I'm supposed to take control of the company. Only it appears that someone wanted to ensure that didn't happen. That's why I needed to get out of Thornwood now, before it's too late to do something about it. I'm just hoping it's not too late already."

The words came out in a rush, then stopped abruptly as though she figured she'd said too much. Once she stopped, she simply lifted her chin and stood there, watching him.

Josh could only stare back at her. He had no idea how he was supposed to respond to a story that outlandish. Bribery? Billion-dollar corporations? A conspiracy hatched by an unknown "someone" against her? It was the stuff of paranoid delusions, created by an unstable mind.

Yet the eyes that met his were clear and focused. She'd related her story calmly and concisely, her voice unwavering. Whatever the veracity of her tale, there wasn't a doubt in his mind that she believed it to be true.

But then, he'd spoken the truth to Aaron that afternoon—he wasn't a psychiatrist. All he had were his instincts to tell him whether or not to believe her, instincts he was no longer certain he could trust.

He could either believe she was the victim of a conspiracy or simply a mental patient who belonged in the institution to which she'd been committed.

And Josh had the sad feeling that in this case the more likely answer was the correct one.

HE DIDN'T BELIEVE HER.

His expression hadn't changed. He had that patient, pleasant look on his face that revealed nothing of his thoughts. She could tell all the same.

Claire swallowed a groan of frustration and forced herself to take the deep breath he'd suggested earlier. She couldn't afford to lose her composure. Her only hope of getting this man on her side was to come across as sane and rational as she knew she was.

If only she hadn't fallen asleep and lost her grip, tumbling back against the side of the trunk when he'd come to a stop. But it had been a long drive, and once the initial adrenaline rush of her escape had worn off, she'd felt the damned fatigue dragging at her. Even now, it pulled at her. Her body trembled, from exhaustion, tension and perhaps the lack of drugs her body was used to receiving by now.

Her stomach twisted with anxiety. Every moment she stood here was another moment she was wasting not getting away. She had to agree with him—it wouldn't take the people at Thornwood long to discover that she was missing. Even now they could be on their way, ready to reclaim her, while she was making the mistake of confiding in this man.

She'd probably said too much. But after four months of speaking to no one, having to keep all this bottled up inside, her story seemed to come out on its own, a raging torrent that couldn't be stopped.

For all the good it had done her.

"You think I sound paranoid," she said knowingly. "And maybe I do. But like they say, it's not paranoia if they really are out to get you."

From the impassive look on his face, he wasn't ready to concede even that point to her.

She saw in his eyes that there was another option. That she really was mentally unbalanced, making up stories of persecution that bore no resemblance to reality.

Trying to think of another way out, she raised a hand to push back her hair.

"What's that?"

She met his gaze, then followed it where he was looking. Her unconscious gesture had caused her sleeve to slide down, revealing her wrist.

Heat flooded her cheeks. Embarrassed, she quickly lowered her arm, pulling the sleeve all the way over her fingers. "It's nothing."

He finally set the wrench down on the floor just behind him and slowly moved closer, reaching out to offer her his hand. "May I see? I'm a doctor. I promise I'll be careful."

It was the gentleness in his voice that broke her. It was so different from the cool indifference and sneering cruelty she'd heard the past few months from the Thornwood staff. She couldn't remember the last time anyone had spoken to her so kindly. Maybe never.

His face matched his voice. His blue eyes were warm with sympathy. The corners of his mouth tilted ever-so-slightly upward in a compassionate smile. Part of her wondered if this was his doctor face, the practiced expression that conveyed just the right note of caring and made his patients feel at ease. The rest of her couldn't help responding to it. It seemed so genuine. *He* seemed so genuine. Up close, she could see the faint beginnings of laugh lines worn into the skin around the corners of his eyes, while not a single line marred his brow. All of which told her this was a man who smiled a lot. Could it be that this wasn't an act, that this was who he really was? Despite her better judgment, she found herself wanting to believe it, as the band of tightness in her chest eased slightly. Her initial impression of him returned in full force, that this was someone she could trust, someone who could help her.

Almost against her will, she found herself lifting her hand and placing it in his.

His fingers were large and surprisingly soft, his touch gentle. A doctor's hands. She stared at a spot on the far wall as he carefully pushed back the sleeve to bare her forearm. She didn't need to look. She knew what was there. Four long bruises on her wrist, with a shorter corresponding one underneath where Hobbs had grabbed her arm roughly a few days ago. There was another one farther up by the elbow that wasn't as dark. It was already starting to heal. She silently underwent his scrutiny as he pored over one arm, then the other. She knew what was there, too. More of the same.

"Who did this to you?"

She lifted one shoulder in a shrug. "An orderly. Not exactly the best care money can buy, huh?"

"Did you tell anyone?"

"Who would I tell? I'm crazy, remember? No one would have believed me. I know how they would have handled it. The squeaky wheel gets an armful of tranquilizers. Problem solved."

"What about visitors? Didn't anyone notice when they came to see you?"

"Nobody ever came to see me," she said flatly.

He didn't say anything for a moment, no doubt torn between following up with the questions that answer raised and all the others he must have.

When he did speak, his tone was even gentler. "So you just took it and let them hurt you?"

She met his stare head-on. "I did what I had to do to survive."

"How bad did it get?"

She looked away again. "Just the bruises. It didn't go any further."

"Are you sure? You said you were drugged quite a bit of the time."

She opened her mouth to deny it, only to stop short. Horror washed over her. She would know if someone had touched her, or worse, while she was out of it, right? Surely her body would let her know.

But as she thought of all those occasions she'd lost time, all the gaps in her memory, all she felt was doubt.

She swallowed hard, a sick feeling in the pit of her stomach. "I don't know," she whispered.

Josh lapsed into silence again, and she fought the urge to check his expression to see what he was thinking. She didn't want his pity, even if that was what it took for him to let her go. She'd spent too much of her life trying to prove she was strong enough, as tough and as smart and as normal as everyone else, to want this man to see her as a victim.

"Come on. Let's go inside."

Claire jerked her head up in surprise. Whatever she'd expected him to say, that hadn't been it. "Are you letting me go?"

"No."

Her wariness returned. "Are you going to call Thornwood?"

He stared at her for a long moment that left her holding

her breath. Then he sighed and shook his head. "No. I won't call them."

She suspected there was an unspoken *yet* at the end of that sentence. Rather than push her luck, she'd take what she could get. There would be time later to argue the rest.

He was already moving away, toward the door that seemed to lead into the house, apparently leaving her to follow. "Let me see if I can find you something to wear. And are you hungry?"

"Actually I'd kill to use the bathroom."

"No problem. And you can clean up if you like."

She answered without thinking. "A shower would be heaven."

She didn't know why she'd said that. It was true, of course. Even though she was free of Thornwood, she wasn't free of its smell. The sterile scent clung to her body, reminding her with every breath she took. Not to mention she'd been lying in a trunk for more than an hour. After enduring the humiliation of sponge baths all this time, standing under the spray of a shower and washing herself, scrubbing the residue of Thornwood off her, seemed like a dream.

But what she needed was to get out of here. Now that he'd let his guard down, maybe she could make a break for it.

Except she'd already come to the conclusion that she wouldn't be able to fight him if he tried to stop her. He was too big, and she was too regrettably weak after four months of the drugs. She hated this feeling. She'd never been this weak in her life, never let herself be, and now here she was, everything she'd never wanted to be.

"I'll get you some towels," he was saying. He had opened the door and was holding it for her.

Whatever she was going to do, it wouldn't involve

staying in the garage. Straightening her shoulders, she closed the distance between them and walked into the house.

The door led into a small kitchen, neat and sparsely furnished. "The bathroom's down here," he said. Moving past her, he led the way down a hall to the left. Framed photographs lined the walls. Curious in spite of herself, she found herself checking the pictures as they passed by. There were photos of Josh posing with an older couple who must be his parents, with groups of guys she imagined were buddies of his, with children who could be nieces and nephews. As would be expected from pictures deemed suitable for framing and displaying, everyone looked happy. In each, Josh's smile shone like a beacon, its warmth as palpable as it was in person.

She couldn't help notice they were all group shots, with no personal one-on-one photos with a wife or girlfriend. Not that it mattered, of course.

He stopped at the bathroom and turned the light on, then opened the next door, which turned out to be a closet. Pulling out a few towels, he handed them to her. "Help yourself to whatever you need. I'll get you some clothes and leave them here outside the door for when you're ready for them."

"Thank you," she murmured, her voice sounding suspiciously husky to her ears. She started to walk into the bathroom, then hesitated, turning back. "You're really not—"

"I'm not going to call Thornwood," he said firmly. "I promise."

Trusting him was a risk, but one she would have to take. Now that she thought about it, there was no way she could go running around in her hospital gown and robe. It was a surefire way to get stopped by the police, and she didn't need that. If he provided her with some normal clothes, she'd be much better off when she did get away from him and out on her own. Plus there was the little fact that she didn't know where they were. Within driving distance of Thornwood, but that covered a lot of ground.

With a tight nod, she ducked her head and stepped into the bathroom, closing the door behind her.

The room was small but clean. Setting the towel on the countertop next to the sink, she found herself facing her reflection in the mirror. She couldn't help but stare. It had been four months since she'd looked at herself. Her face was a little thinner, but not too much so. Her hair hung limply to her shoulders. There were dark shadows beneath her eyes.

It was the eyes themselves she couldn't ignore. Her face was frozen in a familiar mask, cool, refined, revealing nothing. That detachment didn't reach her eyes. There was a vulnerability there she wasn't used to seeing, along with something just as foreign.

Fear.

Suddenly, staring into her own eyes and the undeniable proof they offered of her ordeal, something inside her cracked. All the emotions she'd suppressed, all the anger she'd squelched, all the fear she'd held at bay, came rushing to the surface. A sob tore itself from her throat. She slapped the palm of her hand over her mouth to cover the sound of it and all the ones that followed, the wrenching cries that seemed to rip themselves painfully from someplace deep inside. Her other hand fumbled to turn on the faucet, then gripped the edge of the sink as she did her best to stay on her feet. She couldn't fall apart completely. There was no time. She might be away from Thornwood, but she wasn't clear yet.

Never show weakness.

Her father's words, the mantra she'd taken as her own, echoed in the back of her mind.

Gradually, with practiced efficiency, she pulled herself together, regaining that touted Preston reserve. She inhaled slowly and deeply, remembering her breathing exercises, until the face that stared back at her was tranquil once more, the eyes revealing nothing.

On the other side of the door was a man who momentarily held her fate in his hands. She didn't like the feeling. More important, she wasn't about to cede control that easily. She hadn't gone through all this just to wind up back at Thornwood.

And the man outside or anyone else who tried to stop her would find out just how hard she was willing to fight to prevent that from happening.

Chapter Three

Josh quickly ducked into his bedroom and retrieved a sweatshirt and a pair of sweatpants with a drawstring waist. They'd obviously be big on her, but they were all he had that might come close to fitting. He took them back to the bathroom. "I'm setting the clothes out here," he called.

He heard the water running, but she didn't say anything. Figuring she'd already done more talking than she'd wanted for the moment, he left the clothes in front of the door and moved away.

He'd offered her food, but that would mean going into the kitchen down the hall, and he wasn't sure he wanted to be that far away. He still wouldn't put it past her to try to run. He didn't know where she was going to go when it didn't look like she had any money or ID on her, but obviously she hadn't planned to let that stop her. He doubted it would now.

Instead, he stepped into the living room where he'd be able to hear the bathroom door open when she came out. He didn't bother sitting, knowing there was no point. He wouldn't be able to remain still. He had too much angry energy pounding through his system, too many questions demanding answers.

The memory of the marks on her arms, the knowledge that someone had hurt her, burned through him. Fury roiled in his gut as he thought of what she'd been subjected to. Anyone who would hurt a woman was bad enough, but hurting a seemingly helpless patient who'd been entrusted to their care was unspeakable.

Her story seemed so implausible. How could no one have noticed her injuries? Or had they really not cared? And the idea that she'd simply endured it for three months to preserve her ability to escape… That seemed to indicate either incredible strength or extreme deviousness.

Or desperation, he allowed.

He didn't know how much of her story to believe. The conspiracy theory she'd spun was either too far-fetched to be true, or too far-fetched not to be. But he couldn't deny the evidence of her mistreatment.

The phone rang, breaking into his thoughts. Somehow he knew who it was before he checked the caller ID and saw the number on the screen. After all, he'd predicted it to Claire not long before.

Thornwood.

He hesitated before answering it. He didn't know if he was ready to admit that she was with him, or to commit to lying and saying she wasn't. It would be better if he decided what he was going to do before making either move, but he was nowhere near that point.

The phone rang again. He could just let it go unanswered.

A third ring. The need for an explanation of Claire's story and her injuries overrode his caution. He picked it up.

As expected, it was Aaron. "Josh, I'm sorry to bother you, but I've been trying to reach you for a while now."

He realized he'd never bothered to turn his cell phone

back on when he left Thornwood, then he'd forgotten it in the car after finding Claire. "Oh?"

"We have a bit of a situation here. One of our patients is missing. It appears she attacked an orderly and took off. There's no sign of her on the premises, and as near as we can tell, only three vehicles left the grounds between the time she was last seen and when the front gate was alerted to search all departing vehicles. We've already checked with the other two, and the drivers said they didn't see anyone and their trucks were empty. We were wondering if she somehow managed to get into your car and escape when you left."

Josh zeroed in on the most relevant part of the statement. Claire had attacked an orderly? He felt a moment's pause before remembering what she'd told him. Maybe the orderly had had it coming.

He knew he had to make his choice, to either conceal Claire's whereabouts until he figured out how best to help her, or to reveal her presence.

In the end his desire for answers was too great. "She's here."

He heard Aaron exhale sharply. "That's what we figured. A van has already been dispatched to retrieve her. You're at home, right? They should be there shortly. Do you think you can handle her until they get there? She may be dangerous. The orderly is in pretty rough shape."

"Maybe he deserved to be."

"I'm sorry?"

"I said maybe he deserved to be. And by the way, you can tell the van to turn back. She's not going anywhere until I get an explanation for why she has bruises in varying stages of healing all over her arms, injuries she said an orderly caused."

From his silence, Josh knew he'd caught Aaron completely off guard. After a long moment, Aaron said, "They're probably self-inflicted."

"Unless her hands somehow swelled to twice their normal size, she didn't leave those bruises on her arms."

"Then maybe she convinced someone else to do it to make her more sympathetic when she made her escape."

"That would require some planning. Is there a reason why she would need to escape so badly she'd make such plans ahead of time?"

"She's a patient in a mental health facility, Josh. Sometimes they don't want to be here."

"Aaron, I saw this woman when I first arrived at Thornwood this afternoon. She looked completely unaware of her surroundings, like she could barely lift her head. According to her, she's been faking her drugged state for months. Yet no one on the staff noticed or thought it was strange that a supposedly catatonic patient had bruises all over her?"

"Obviously there was some kind of oversight—"

"Obviously," Josh repeated, unable to keep the scorn from his voice. "What the hell kind of operation are you people running there? Because, I have to say, this kind of contradicts the whole spiel about a first-class facility you were feeding me this afternoon."

"As I said, there must have been some kind of oversight. You can rest assured this will be investigated—"

"What's her diagnosis?"

The sudden change in topic seemed to have caught Aaron off guard again. "I'm not—"

"You're telling me that she attacked someone, that she did this to herself, that she had someone else do it, and that she's devious enough to plot to make herself look sympathetic once she escaped. What exactly is she suffering from that would lead you to believe she's capable of this behavior?" Aaron's silence lasted a beat too long. "Do you know anything about this patient, or are you just throwing a bunch of theories around to cover the asses of you and your colleagues?"

Aaron took on a deeply affronted tone. "I'm not personally familiar with her case, but I know Dr. Emmons himself is in charge of her care and he is deeply concerned for her well-being."

Emmons. That much lined up with her story. "Or deeply concerned with the truth of her treatment at Thornwood not being revealed? Maybe even the reason she's there in the first place?"

"This is ridiculous. I don't know what she's told you—"

"Enough that I'm not about to let her go back there."

"Josh, the woman needs to be in a psychiatric facility!"

"And you say this as an expert on her condition?"

"I may not know the specifics, but I know she's mentally ill."

"And yet, at the moment she sounds a great deal more rational and coherent than you do."

Aaron's voice turned cold enough to freeze the phone lines between them. "The decision is not yours to make. A team from Thornwood is already on its way to retrieve her. Make no mistake about it, if you prevent them from doing so in any way, we will contact the authorities and report you for unlawfully removing her from our care. Given your current situation, do you really need that kind of trouble?"

It was just another sign that Aaron had never really known him. If he had, he would know Josh had never responded well to being threatened. He had no trouble matching the frostiness in Aaron's tone. "Tell me something, Harris. Is that why you called me about the job? Because you thought my situation was so grim I'd be desperate enough to sell out the way you seem to have done?"

The telling silence that echoed across the line was answer enough.

"I figured as much." He hung up the phone without another word.

"You said you wouldn't call."

Josh turned to find Claire standing in the doorway behind him, her hair damp from the shower. Betrayal rang in her voice.

"I didn't. He called me."

He read the uncertainty on her face, as though she wasn't quite sure whether or not to believe him. She was wearing his sweats, virtually swimming in them. He could still see that every line of her body was tense. She looked as wary as a deer that sensed imminent danger, ready to bolt at any moment.

He forced himself to relax his expression into something more reassuring and offered her a smile. "Do you want something to eat?"

"What did he say?"

There was no point in lying. She'd learn the truth soon enough. "They figured out you must have left with me. They're already on their way."

As he anticipated, she immediately turned toward the doorway.

He moved to intercept her. "Where are you going to go? You don't have any money or identification, do you?"

"It doesn't matter. I'm just not going back there."

"I didn't say I would let them take you."

"And how exactly are you going to stop them? You don't have any authority over me."

"According to you, neither do they. Legally, at least."

"That hasn't stopped them so far."

"We can go to the police right now and explain how you're being hurt there. Once they see your injuries, they won't make you go back."

"You don't know that. Besides, Milton has plenty of police connections. I know for a fact he plays golf with the police commissioner."

Josh frowned, trying to follow her train of thought. "Who's Milton?"

Impatience flashed across her face. "Milton Vaughn is the current CEO of PAD. My father left him in control after he died."

"And you think he's responsible for having you institutionalized?"

"According to my father's will, Milton is only to remain in charge until I inherit the controlling shares of the company. He's the only one with a motive to pay someone to have me committed, and he could have told the police anything when Emmons told him I escaped."

"Maybe he hasn't had a chance. Maybe Emmons hasn't told him yet."

"I can't take that chance. Even if they don't send me back to Thornwood, they could ship me off to another mental hospital, and I'm not about to risk that. I know you don't believe me, and you're only helping me because of this—" she lifted her arms to demonstrate what she meant "—but I don't belong in a rubber room somewhere, and the only way I'm going to find out how I ended up in one in the first place is to stay out of any others."

"It might not be the worst thing to talk to another psychiatrist," he said carefully. "If you truly aren't mentally ill, another doctor should be able to recognize that."

"Do you really think it's that easy to escape the taint of mental illness once someone's put that label on you?" She shook her head. "Besides, that isn't my only reason. I know you don't believe me, but I can't afford to have this get out, especially to the press. If someone conspired to have me institutionalized, the media would have a field day with the story. The embarrassment it could cause to the company could be irreparable. I may not be in charge at the moment, but I intend to be in the near future. Even if I didn't, I have a responsibility to the employees and shareholders to keep this whole ridiculous episode from hurting the company."

This wasn't the terrified woman who'd faced off with him in the garage, nor the embarrassed one who'd looked away when he examined her bruises. She'd switched into another gear entirely. Josh couldn't help looking at her differently and reassessing his opinion of her. Her spine was straight, her shoulders squared, her head held high. Her tone of voice was soft, but firm, with the command of someone used to being in charge. Her claim that she was soon to be the head of an international corporation suddenly was entirely believable. What was hard to believe was that the woman currently standing before him would ever let herself be victimized. Then again, it was easy to imagine this woman doing exactly what she felt she had to do under any circumstances.

Before he could respond, the soft squeal of a braking vehicle sounded from the street out front.

Her bravado faltered slightly, and she paled. "They're here."

"Hold on," he said when it looked like she was on the verge of taking off the way they'd come in. "We don't know that." He quickly crossed to the front window and peeked out through the blinds.

A white van had pulled up in front of his house. It was unmarked, but he knew immediately where it was from. He didn't miss the fact that it completely blocked his driveway. Cutting off any possible escape.

He shook his head. Claire's conspiracy theories were starting to get to him. He was getting as paranoid as she was.

As he watched, a car pulled up behind the van. A man slowly climbed out of the driver's seat. The three men exiting the van seemed to expect him, acknowledging his presence. He made no move to join them.

A chill rolled down the back of Josh's neck. Four men seemed a little excessive for one woman. Did they really think it would take all of them to retrieve her?

It's not paranoia if they really are out to get you.

It was the man who climbed out of the second vehicle who caught Josh's attention. He could immediately tell there was something different about this man, the way he carried himself. He held back as the others moved toward the house, his stance watchful, his expression a stony mask.

As Josh watched, the man pushed back the side of his jacket, his hand reflexively checking an object that was briefly exposed in that moment.

The sight propelled Josh into action. He turned away from the window. "We have to get out of here."

Relief flashed across Claire's face until she saw his expression. "What's wrong?"

He was already across the room, herding her toward the

hallway with a soft but insistent hand at the small of her back. "Can you think of any reason why they'd have guns?"

"You mean tranquilizer guns?"

"Not unless Smith & Wesson started making those."

He felt her flinch, but didn't stop to react, just kept moving. Despite what Aaron had said, he had to believe she wasn't violent unless provoked. When he'd led her to the bathroom, he'd kept his guard up in case she decided to attack him when his back was turned. She hadn't. Which made the four men outside seem like overkill.

Or something more sinister.

He could try to turn them away, but he suspected the fourth man was there to ensure they didn't take no for an answer.

They made it back to the kitchen. She started for the garage. "Not that way," he told her, motioning to another door. "Through here."

Grabbing his keys from the counter, he stepped out into the backyard and moved to open the gate. This side of the house wasn't visible from the front, but something told him he couldn't count on their visitors not circling the house. They still had to hurry. Once the gate was open, he crossed to where he'd left the Harley. He looked back to find Claire had stopped just outside the door.

"Does that thing even run?" she asked doubtfully.

From the toolbox he'd left out and the various dirty rags around, it was obvious he'd been working on the motorcycle. "I sure hope so. Either way, we're about to find out." He climbed onto the bike and raised a brow in question at her. "You coming?"

She didn't hesitate further, breaching the distance in a few quick strides. Bracing her hand on his shoulder, she swung onto the back of the Harley behind him. Her arms automatically went around his middle.

The sensation of having her so close, her limbs wrapped around him, sent a jolt through him he did his best to ignore. As soon as she was on board, he kicked the engine to life. Sure enough, it gave an encouraging roar that left no doubt of its ability to get them out of there fast.

Seemingly reassured, Claire tightened her grip and leaned close, her breasts tight against his back. Quickly attributing the tremor that quaked through him to the rumble of the bike, he leaned forward and sent them roaring off into the night.

Chapter Four

Ahmed waited until the group from Thornwood drove away, heading back to inform their boss that they were as incompetent as he was, before breaking into the house. It was pathetically simple. The home's security system wouldn't keep out a determined child.

Once inside, he slowly made his way through the rooms, searching for any clue to where the doctor might have taken the woman. In truth, this mission was beneath him. He had several men loyal to their cause who were capable of finding one woman.

But few of those devout men would enjoy what they could do once they found her as much as he would.

He allowed himself a moment to savor the burst of anticipation before refocusing on the task at hand. If they had gone to the police, then all was likely lost. He suspected they had not. She was from a wealthy family, connected to a prominent company. She wouldn't want the attention. At the very least, he had to proceed as though they hadn't until he knew otherwise.

If she tried contacting her family, he would be informed. The most obvious places she might choose to go were all covered. That left him to learn of the places the doctor might choose for them.

As he searched, he studied the man's home, gathering an impression of the man who lived here, all the better to understand his quarry. It was clear he lived alone. The house was small, the furnishings basic.

A simple man.

A man who had no idea what he was interfering with.

A man who shouldn't prove to be much of an adversary.

Pictures lined the walls, displaying a multitude of faces, each of them a possible ally the doctor might turn to. Even if Ahmed was able to identify all of them, the sheer number made it unlikely he would be able to locate the correct one.

Arriving in a home office, he found an address book sitting next to the phone. A quick flip through its pages revealed names, addresses and phone numbers, all meticulously documented. Perhaps the doctor would turn to one of the people listed. He tucked the book into his coat pocket.

He was about to leave the room when a business card tacked to a board above the desk caught his attention. He didn't question why the man had it. All that mattered was that he did.

Reaching up, he pulled it from the board and studied the name of the place embossed on the card. A smile curved the corners of his mouth, instinct telling him this was what he was looking for.

He had heard of such places, of course. A place intended to hide women.

Perhaps even this one.

COME ON. PICK UP. PLEASE pick up.

Claire clutched the phone to her ear and counted the

rings on the other end of the line. After four of them, the answering machine picked up, exactly as it had the last time she'd called.

She hung up without saying a word.

"Still no answer?"

Her heart sinking to the pit of her stomach, Claire shook her head. "She's not answering her home phone or her cell. She's either out or she's screening."

Her back was to him, but she felt Josh watching her from across the kitchen. "You didn't want to leave a message?"

"I don't know if I should." Karen was the one person in the world she trusted enough to contact, but Claire didn't know who else had access to her messages. She couldn't risk leaving a callback number for the same reason, and had only used the phone once Josh had assured her that his friends' private number was blocked on caller ID. Besides, what she really needed was to speak to Karen directly, not her answering machine or voice mail.

Claire checked the clock on the wall, calculating how long it had been since her last attempt, wondering how long she should wait before trying again. Karen should be able to tell her what was happening at the company, what everyone had been told about her disappearance, more information that would help her assess her situation and figure out how to proceed. That is if Karen was still working there. What if they'd fired her? Even then, it was vital that Claire speak with her. Maybe Josh was right. Maybe she should have left a message.

Propping her elbows on the kitchen table, Claire rubbed her fingertips into the center of her forehead, as though that would alleviate the pounding inside her skull. So many questions, so many things she needed to know. At the same time, she had important choices to make, and she couldn't risk making the wrong ones. One false step and the consequences could be dire.

She didn't even notice Josh's approach until he set a bowl on the table in front of her.

"I made you some soup."

She fluttered a hand in dismissal. "I'm not hungry."

"When's the last time you ate? You need to keep your strength up if you're going to get to the bottom of all this."

She shot him a wry glance. "Doctor's orders?"

He folded his arms over that very wide chest, his expression serious. "If necessary."

With a sigh, she picked up the spoon already lying on the placemat and dipped it into the bowl. She stirred the soup but made no move to bring it to her lips. "I'll try her again in a little while."

"Somehow I doubt you'll be awake that long."

Just hearing him say the words made her feel the fatigue in her bones more strongly. "I can't stay here all night."

"Why not? You're safe here. Since you used my cell, it's unlikely anyone will figure out where we are."

"What if your friends come home?"

He eyed her curiously. "I told you. They're out of the country. Don't you remember?"

Had he? Maybe when they'd first arrived, but she hadn't been paying attention, so focused on her need to call Karen that nothing else had mattered. And though she'd never admit it, the weariness dragging at her did make it hard to concentrate.

Trying to distract herself, she glanced around the elaborately equipped kitchen. The house where he'd brought them was an elegant two-story in a tony neighborhood. It was the kind of house where it seemed likely the owners wouldn't want anyone coming inside with their shoes on, let alone staying while they were gone. She almost felt uncomfortable sitting there in his giant sweats.

"Are you sure your friends won't mind us being here?"

"If they were here, they would have taken us in, no questions asked. And I'll make sure to leave everything the way we found it when we go. Which is why you shouldn't have any reservations about staying here."

"I can't waste any more time sitting around."

"You need to rest. You look like you're about to pass out at any moment. You just about gave me a heart attack on the way here every time your grip slipped and I thought you were going to let go."

That was odd. The whole ride over she'd held on as tight as she could, so much so it hadn't felt like she could possibly get any closer to him. She'd wrapped her arms so firmly around his midsection she'd practically been able to feel the outline of his abs. More than once she'd closed her eyes and laid her head against the broad expanse of his back, unable to get enough of how reassuringly solid he felt. It had been so long since she'd been that close to another person. Even with everything so uncertain, or maybe because of it, she'd needed that closeness for as long as it lasted.

Not that she was about to admit any of that to him.

The memory brought heat to her cheeks. She lowered her head, studiously avoiding his eyes. "If I were you I would have been more worried that the motorcycle could fall apart at any moment. That's what it felt like was going to happen."

"It got us here, didn't it?"

"Tell me, do you have something against motor vehicles made in the last two decades?"

"Hey, that bike is a classic."

"And your car?"

His grin turned sheepish. "Okay, the car is not. I've had it since I was sixteen, and even back then it wasn't much to look at."

"So why don't you get a new one?"

"Because if I had a nicer car, I might be tempted to drive it, and I prefer the Harley. There's nothing like it. The exhilaration, the freedom. You just don't get that from a car. I can't get it out on the open road as much as I'd like, so I have to settle for using it to get around the city every day. It helps me clear my head and keeps me—" He stopped abruptly, clamping his mouth shut with a trace of embarrassment.

"Sane?" she finished, somewhat amused in spite of herself. "I'm afraid if I started riding a motorcycle, it would have only made people think I was crazy long ago."

Tonight was the first time she'd ever been on a motorcycle, but she couldn't disagree with his description. The exhilaration. The freedom. She'd felt it rushing through her veins as he'd steered them through the darkened streets.

Or had it been the man she was riding with?

She thought of her nice, safe Volvo. Not exactly the most freeing or exhilarating vehicle on the planet. Of course, she couldn't think of anything in her life she could describe with those terms.

She frowned. It seemed like an eternity since she'd last driven her car. Was it still in her parking space in the garage? Did she even still have a parking space? Was her condo still hers? And her belongings?

The thoughts brought back everything he'd momentarily distracted her from. The flood of memory was disconcerting. She couldn't believe she'd managed to forget about the situation at hand, even for a moment. The man was dangerously easy to talk to. Maybe he should have been a shrink after all.

A shudder rolled through her at the idea. Perish the thought.

Newly refocused, Claire rechecked the clock. How long had it been since her last attempt to reach Karen? "Maybe I should try my friend again."

"Look, the friend I called is already on her way. At least let her check you out. She's a doctor."

"I thought you were a doctor."

"I am. I figured you'd be more comfortable with a woman. And I believe you said something about not wanting me to be your doctor."

That much was true. If he saw her naked, she didn't want it to be in a medical situation.

She shook her head to try to clear her thoughts. Woozy. That's what she was. Her brain was still muddled from the drugs. That had to be it. That was where all these strange, inappropriate thoughts were coming from. They didn't make sense otherwise.

They certainly had nothing to do with the way he looked standing there, so big and brawny, the light deepening the blue of his eyes. With his arms folded over his chest, his biceps bulged in the sleeves of his dress shirt. He looked so strong. That initial impression she'd had of him as a man capable of taking on the world came back to her. He looked even more formidable up close. And far more tempting.

As she watched, a shadow fell over his features. His eyes pored over her face, an unreadable expression on his.

"They said you attacked an orderly," he said softly.

She lifted her chin and met his eyes straight on. "That's right."

"Is he the one who's been hurting you?"

"Yes."

He nodded tersely. "Then good."

She cocked her head. "And if he hadn't been?"

"We all do what we have to do to survive, right?"

He was only paraphrasing what she'd said earlier, but the sound of those words coming out of that mouth, spoken by this man, was so incongruous she narrowed her eyes and studied him more closely. He'd said *we,* lumping himself in with her. As if he could possibly know what it was like to be so desperate.

Yet there was a strange, sad note in his voice, completely at odds with her image of him, that almost made her think he knew what he was talking about.

A light tap on the front door broke the silence. Her tension skyrocketed and she bolted to her feet, ready to move if necessary.

Looking considerably less concerned, Josh moved toward the hallway. "That must be Beth."

"What if it's not?"

"Then I'll get rid of whoever it is. Stay here."

Normally such an order would have rankled her, but it came out as a casual comment rather than a demand. She still didn't retake her seat, not about to let down her guard.

She listened carefully, her nerves on edge, as Josh opened the door and greeted the caller. A woman's voice responded. Claire couldn't make out the exact words, but their tone told her their comments were friendly.

The voices gradually came closer, the words growing

into coherence. "Boyfriend or husband?" the woman murmured to Josh just before they stepped into the room.

"Neither. It's…complicated."

A tall, full-figured redhead followed Josh through the doorway, a black medical bag in one hand and a brown shopping bag cradled in her other arm. Her face softened into a sympathetic smile when she saw Claire.

A similar look had just about melted Claire earlier when Josh had given it to her. It was no less kind coming from this woman, yet something about it rubbed Claire the wrong way. It wasn't the first time in her life people had looked at her like that, with sympathy, with pity. She hadn't liked it before. She didn't like it now.

"Claire, this is my colleague, Dr. Beth Lambert," Josh said, giving her last name the French pronunciation. "Beth, this is Claire."

"Nice to meet you," Claire said politely.

"Same here."

"There's a guest bedroom at the top of the stairs," Josh said. "I thought that might be a good place for the exam." Then, as though just realizing she hadn't necessarily agreed to this, he looked to Claire. "If that's all right with you," he added quickly.

She didn't have the energy to take offense at his high-handedness. This woman's presence and her reason for being here brought back all the terrible possibilities of what might have been done to her without her knowledge at Thornwood. Her skin began to crawl and she had to swallow hard over a lump that suddenly formed in her throat.

She nodded tightly. "Might as well find out how bad the damage is."

They both gave her that sympathetic look. She turned

away, not wanting to see it, and headed down the hall for the stairs. She heard Beth exchange a few muffled words with Josh before following.

The bedroom was the first door at the top of the stairs, exactly where he'd said it would be. Like the rest of the house, it was vast and beautifully furnished. Claire stepped inside. Beth moved past her, setting her bags on the bed and opening the medical case.

Standing stiffly by the door, Claire watched her movements. She knew she should probably start to undress, but despite the necessity of this exam, she suddenly wasn't ready to expose her injuries to anyone else.

Instead, she latched on to something to say. "What did you mean when you asked about a boyfriend or husband?"

The woman paused and gave her an apologetic smile. "I'm sorry. I wasn't trying to invade your privacy. It's just that I know Josh from a family shelter downtown. We both volunteer there, and nearly all of the women we see there have been mistreated by their significant others. When Josh called, I assumed this was a similar situation."

Claire nodded, strangely discomfited by this newfound knowledge. So Josh wasn't a stranger at coming to the aid of women in trouble. Was that how he saw her? As just another victim in need of help? She wasn't sure that was much better than having him think she was crazy.

"Do many men volunteer there? For some reason, perhaps erroneously, I always thought it would generally be women working at a shelter."

"You're not wrong. The shelter does have a predominantly female staff. Many of the women who come for help aren't entirely comfortable around men, especially one of

Josh's size, given their own experiences. But he just has a way of putting people at ease, especially the kids. Many of the children have suffered at the hands of fathers or other men in their lives as well, but they really respond to Josh. Most of them are hungry for some healthy male attention, and he's able to give that to them, if only for a little while."

Thinking of her own reaction to Josh, Claire found it all too easy to believe. His natural warmth had broken straight through her defenses. She could imagine how a child would respond to him. Even if Beth hadn't told her so, she knew instinctively that he would be good with kids.

For some reason, she was reminded of Blake, her not-so-lamented former fiancé, who'd been eager to have children with her. She'd known for a long time that she couldn't have them. She'd mentioned adoption as an alternative possibility, but he'd only been interested in having biological children with her. Eventually she'd figured out that he didn't really want a child. As a rising young executive at PAD, he'd wanted a permanent link to her family or, more specifically, the company, even in case of divorce. Their entire relationship had been nothing more than a way to cement his position at the company. Ending things with him hadn't exactly been a challenge.

She watched Beth pull a camera from the shopping bag and set it on the bedside table. "What's that for?"

"To document your injuries if you want to press charges. Even if you don't want to immediately, it's good to have a record in case you change your mind."

"That won't be necessary. I can't press charges." It was bad enough that another person had been told what happened to her. She couldn't imagine telling the police, testifying to it in court, having the whole sordid tale reported in the press. The experience was humiliating enough as it was.

Beth met her eyes with a firm, no-nonsense expression. "Whoever did this to you should be punished. You can't let him get away with it."

"I know. It's just..." Claire finished lamely when no other word came to mind, "complicated."

Beth's lips thinned into a tight smile, her expression rueful. "It always is," she said sadly. "All right. I'll spare you the lectures. Let's see what I can do to help."

MICK AND AMY KELLER HAD spared no expense when it came to their home. Two successful professionals—an investment banker and an architect—with thriving careers, they could afford to live in style. As such, their home was designed for comfort. In all the times he'd visited Mick, an old college roommate, and his wife at their house, Josh had never spent an uncomfortable moment there.

Until now.

The minutes seemed to stretch out interminably as he waited for Beth in the kitchen. He couldn't even pace, not wanting to make a sound that would prevent him from hearing her return. Instead, he braced himself against the kitchen counter and listened closely, every muscle on edge.

As soon as he heard the door upstairs open and close, he snapped to attention. Fighting the urge to meet her at the bottom of the stairs, he stayed where he was and poured her a cup of coffee.

He'd just replaced the pot when Beth stepped into the kitchen.

He handed her the cup. "Well?"

Taking a healthy swallow, she shook her head. "She hasn't been abused sexually. It appears she hasn't had any kind of sexual activity in quite some time."

He exhaled sharply as relief shot through him. "At least that's something."

"It just leaves the bruises on her arms and shoulders, not to mention the needle marks on her arms. But I'm guessing you already knew about those."

He nodded once.

"She doesn't strike me as an addict, which means either she's a hospital patient or whatever she's on was likely administered against her will."

"Or both."

He'd made the comment without thinking, unable to hold back the angry mutter. Beth's brows went up. He shook his head at the unspoken question.

Beth frowned, and he could practically see her biting her tongue. "She says she doesn't want to press charges. Not that I'm surprised. She comes from money, right? Or she's somebody important?"

"How can you tell?"

Beth shrugged. "Experience. Something about the way she carries herself. She has the bearing of someone with status, societal or monetary."

He'd had the same impression himself. He was still glad to hear Beth's feeling matched his own. It certainly added credence to Claire's story, unless she really was deluded enough to affect such a persona.

Lost in his own thoughts, he failed to respond to Beth's comment. He didn't notice until she sighed. "Look, I don't know how you met this woman and I have a feeling you're not going to tell me."

"You're probably better off not knowing. I don't want to drag you into this any more than you are now."

She grimaced. "Aren't you supposed to be staying out of trouble yourself?"

"What would you expect me to do? Not help her?"

"No, that's the last thing I'd expect from you. And right now you need to help her by talking her into going to the police. I may not know the circumstances of how you found her, but it's clear that she's in trouble and that she trusts you. You know she has to report this."

"I also know better than anyone that a woman who doesn't want to talk to the police isn't going to."

"True. And look how well that situation turned out for you."

They stared at each other for a moment. Her gaze was pointed, but sympathetic. He couldn't disagree with what she was saying. "I can't stand by and do nothing. It's hard enough to get her to agree to let me help her at all. But as long as I can help her, I will."

Beth shook her head, a pained expression briefly flashing over her face. "I hope you know what you're doing."

Josh released a humorless laugh. "You and me both."

She drained the last of her coffee, and he walked her back to the front door.

Beth stopped in the doorway and gave him one last look. "Be careful, Josh."

"I will."

Her worried expression never wavered, but she still turned and walked out the door.

Locking up behind her, Josh headed up the stairs to the bedroom and knocked softly on the closed door. "Claire?"

When there was no response, he knocked again. No

sound came from within. He pushed the door open and peeked inside. Claire lay on the bed, already asleep. He spotted the clothes Beth must have brought for her sitting at the end of the bed. Instead of putting them on, Claire was wearing his sweats again.

She was curled up on her side, her hands knotted into fists, as though she was ready to lash out and fight at any moment. He had a feeling that was exactly the case. The light from the open door fell over her face, illuminating the fierceness in her expression even in sleep. He felt a sharp stab of anger in his gut. She'd been through hell in that place. Even though she was finally out of there, she hadn't come close to leaving it behind. He knew it would be a long time, if ever, before she did.

Claire shifted fitfully, and he could tell she wasn't sleeping deeply. He was almost surprised she hadn't woken when he'd knocked. Rather than risk waking her, he silently backed out of the room and left the door open so he'd hear her if she called out. He'd meant what he said earlier. She needed to rest. It might not be the best sleep she'd ever gotten, but any at all would still do her a world of good.

With Claire settled and the most pressing business dealt with for the moment, he took a deep breath for the first time in what seemed like forever. He just had to figure out what the hell to do next.

Beth hadn't told him anything he didn't already know. The police were best equipped to deal with Claire's situation. He also knew he wasn't about to betray her trust by going to them without consulting her. He would never get it back, and with the trouble she was in, she needed someone she could rely on.

Normally he had several buddies on the force he trusted

who might keep this quiet for the time being. But given his current situation, he had a feeling he didn't have much credibility with them at the moment. The cops he knew might like him, but they wouldn't put their careers on the line by getting sucked into another of his problems, even if his buddies did believe him.

They really were on their own.

They.

It took him a moment to realize he'd thought of them as a combined unit. She wasn't on her own. They were.

As soon as the idea sank in, he had to acknowledge the rightness of it. The moment he'd responded to Aaron's threat of calling the police by hanging up on him, Josh had cast his fate with Claire's. They were in this together now.

Beth probably would have lectured him about getting personally involved, but he knew it was too late. He already was involved. There was no way around that.

Which meant he needed to know exactly what he was involved in.

He wished he could hop online and start finding some answers. He needed to know more about this woman and what they were facing. Unfortunately, Mick and Amy never went anywhere without their laptops, even when they were ostensibly supposed to be on vacation, and they didn't have a desktop computer. He wasn't about to leave Claire alone to track one down. She might need him. Even if she didn't, he'd told her she was safe here. He was going to make sure that remained true.

He felt his resolve harden into a lump in the pit of his stomach. Nothing was going to happen to this woman. Not on his watch.

He had enough blood on his hands.

Chapter Five

Ahmed passed the night in his vehicle, his attention focused on the building across the street from where he'd parked. A shelter, it was called. A spot for American women who didn't know their place and failed to obey their husbands, then ran away from the consequences.

And perhaps a place to hide a woman being sought by someone other than her husband.

But in the course of the long night, the man and the woman had not come here. Which meant either that they had arrived before he had, coming straight from the house, or they were not coming at all.

Just before dawn, as he was considering his next move, the front door opened. A woman stepped outside, a tall creature with red hair. She was a disgrace, carrying herself like a man, too much pride in her stance. He'd seen her arrive late the night before. She'd managed to get inside before he could intercept her. If the woman he sought was here, this woman would likely know.

He quickly stepped from his vehicle, his weapon in hand, and crossed the street in the shadows, stopping outside the fence surrounding the property.

Within seconds, she stepped through the gate. He knew immediately when she sensed his presence. She didn't stop and look around. She was too clever for that. No, her posture gave her away. Her spine straightened the slightest bit, an indication she'd suddenly gone on guard. She missed a step, her stride stuttering for just a moment. Her hand reached down to slip into her bag.

He didn't give her a chance to retrieve her weapon. Bursting into motion, he caught her with an arm around her neck and pulled her back into the shadows. The sound of something clattering against the pavement suggested she'd dropped whatever she'd been reaching for. Pepper spray, perhaps.

He felt her open her mouth to scream. Before she could, he tightened his arm around her neck and pushed the barrel of his weapon into the side of her head with his other hand. From the way she swallowed hard, she recognized what it was. Good.

"If you move, if you make any sound, I will shoot you. Do you understand?"

After a long moment, she nodded. Fear radiated from her. He could practically smell it. A thrill flooded his veins and it was all he could do not to smile.

Did she think she would be safe if she obeyed? Because he'd made no such promise.

How long had it been since he'd killed such a woman, such a disgusting, wicked creature?

Too long, the answer whispered through his mind.

Keeping the gun pressed tight to her head, he released his arm from around her neck and reached into his pocket. "Look at this picture." He pushed the photograph in front of her face. "I am looking for this woman. Is she here?"

It was a simple question, one she should have no trouble answering. Yet she hesitated. He pondered the reason for this. Was she not certain of the answer? Or was she considering lying to hide the woman's presence here?

"Answer me." He drove the weapon harder into her skull, eliciting a satisfying little gasp from her. "Is she here?"

"Hey, what's going on out there?"

The shrill voice distracted him for just a second. His gaze flicked to the doorway of the building, where someone now stood. No doubt the woman who'd called out.

His brief lapse in concentration cost him. The gun wavered. A second later he felt the sharp jab of an elbow in his gut. Before he could adjust, the woman he held grabbed his arm and doubled over, flipping him right over her head with an outraged scream.

He landed on his back with a crash that knocked the wind from his lungs. The jolt didn't stop him from regaining his bearings. Almost as soon as he landed, he rolled to his right. The kick she'd no doubt aimed at his side just missed him, close enough for him to feel the whoosh of air as her foot flew by. He kept rolling, twisting over and over until he was safely out of range, then bound to his feet in a low crouch.

The gun was still in his hand. It must have been the only thing that kept her from pursuing him. They stared at each other across the distance, and he could see the hatred in her face, nearly as fierce as what he felt pounding through his body. The hand holding his weapon was already rising, ready to take aim, eager to fulfill the desire flooding him. To blow her head clean off. To rid the world of one more decadent American whore.

He didn't get the chance to make that sweet wish a

reality. She spun on her heel and raced toward the building, waving her arms to signal the other woman, who seemed to have come closer, back inside. Where she most likely thought they'd be safe.

He could have laughed at that thought. They weren't safe. None of them were.

This whole degenerate country would learn that soon enough.

He longed to follow them inside, to prove to them just how wrong they were. There was no time. Even if he did manage to get inside, it was likely someone within had already summoned the police.

Straightening, he glanced around quickly to see if anyone had noticed the scene and was watching. He saw no one. The street remained empty in the pale light of dawn.

Satisfied, he returned to his vehicle. Claire Preston might not be here, but she had to be somewhere. He would find her, he had no doubt of that. If anything, his task had become easier with the start of this new day. He no longer had to concern himself with finding and detaining her until the time was right.

Now she could simply die.

CLAIRE SLOWLY, PAINFULLY, came awake, feeling like she was swimming upward from the bottom of a huge pool of mud, struggling to break the surface. Her head throbbed, all of her limbs felt as though they weighed about a hundred pounds, and it seemed so much easier to remain in her current state than to fight her way out of it.

But something in the back of her mind prodded her forward, the reminder that there was something important she needed to be doing....

Somehow she managed to pry her eyelids apart. She peered blearily around the unfamiliar room, wincing at the sunlight flooding the space. It was too bright. She gradually made the connection that this must mean it was late.

Her gaze finally fell on a clock next to the bed. It was two in the afternoon. Strange. She never slept so late.

It all came back to her in a rush. Everything that had happened. Everything she needed to be doing.

She needed to reach Karen. She had to figure out what was going on. What was the matter with her? Four months of waiting to get out of Thornwood, and now that she was free, she was wasting her time sleeping?

There was a bathroom adjoining the bedroom. She used the facilities but avoided the shower, no matter how much it beckoned to her. There was no time. Changing quickly into some of the clothes Beth had brought her, she headed downstairs.

She found Josh in the kitchen, watching a small TV on the counter. He looked up as she entered the room, his expression automatically easing into a smile. At the same time, his eyes quickly surveyed her in one sweeping glance from head to foot, a clinical gleam in them. She wondered what he saw. If she looked even close to how she felt, it couldn't be a pretty picture.

He, on the other hand, looked even better than she remembered. His thick blond hair fell over his forehead with that tousled look some people paid their hairstylists a fortune for, but which she suspected came naturally to him. He was clean-shaven and freshly dressed, looking ready to take on whatever the world threw at him. For one brief, irrational moment she resented his vitality. The way her head was pounding, it felt like she'd gone four rounds with the world and was on the verge of going down for the count.

"How do you feel?" he asked.

"Fine," she lied.

"No tremors? No dizziness?"

She frowned. She might not be feeling her best, but those weren't among her problems. "No. Why?"

"If they've been keeping you drugged for months, you'll probably start suffering through withdrawal once you're no longer receiving the dosage."

"Great. Something to look forward to. Why didn't you wake me up?"

"You needed the rest. Doctor's orders, remember?"

"Eight hours would have been plenty."

"Obviously your body didn't agree. Do you want something to eat?" Without waiting for an answer, he moved toward the refrigerator.

"I don't have time." Her eyes drifted to the phone. It was the middle of the workday. She most likely wouldn't be able to reach Karen at home. Could she risk calling her at work?

"Do you have time to pass out?"

She speared him with a glance. Last night she may have been too tired and weak to fight his high-handedness, but that was no longer the case. "Look, you're not my mother or, as we established last night, my doctor. I appreciate the help you've given me, but I don't need to be treated like a child. I've had more than enough of that lately."

He dipped his head in acknowledgement. "You're right. I'm sorry. That wasn't my intention."

She watched him pull a couple of eggs from the refrigerator and set them on the counter. "And yet you still seem to be cooking."

"I was apologizing for my tone, but I stand by the message, and it has nothing to do with treating you like a child. Adults need to eat, too. You barely had any of that soup last night. If I had to guess, I'd say you haven't really eaten anything in close to twenty-four hours, am I right?"

"It wouldn't have been so long if you'd woken me earlier," she noted.

"I could have woken you at the crack of dawn and you'd still be giving me this argument."

She decided not to acknowledge the comment rather than admit that he was right. From the satisfied sound he made in his throat, she suspected he figured it out anyway.

Needing to get off her feet, she sank onto one of the counter stools. In the background, she could hear him setting a pan on the stove and turning on the burner. Her stomach gave a soft rumble. She was hungry. She was also right; she didn't have time to sit here doing nothing.

The phone was a few feet away on the counter. As she reached for it, her gaze fell on the television he'd been watching. He had it tuned to a local midday news broadcast.

"I've been watching the news all morning," he explained, as though she'd asked. "There's been no mention of your escape from Thornwood. Aaron said they would notify the authorities if I didn't hand you over. If that were the case, don't you think the police would have gotten the word out?"

"Not if my family didn't want the embarrassment of admitting I was in a mental institution."

"Or if you had been held there illegally in the first place."

A small bit of hope blooming in her chest, she eyed him curiously. "Does that mean you believe me?"

He looked up from the stove where he was stirring the eggs and stared at her for a long moment. For the life of her, she couldn't tell what he was thinking. A knot of tension formed in her throat.

"Yes," he said finally. "I believe you."

The knot loosened. Relief poured through her system. It was probably silly. She didn't know this man. It shouldn't matter what he thought. But then, maybe that's exactly why it did. Having just one person believe her, someone who didn't know anything about her and had made up his own mind despite the outlandishness of her story, suddenly made her feel worlds better. Because if she could convince him, she might be able to convince other people, too, and the truth might win out after all.

But that wouldn't happen as long as she continued to sit here.

She picked up the phone. "Then you understand why it's so important for me to figure out what's going on."

"Go ahead and call your friend. I'll give you a lift wherever you want to go. We'll even take one of the cars in the garage so you won't have to worry about the Harley falling apart under us, especially since we had to leave the helmets back at my place."

Her fingers stilled above the buttons she'd been about to start dialing. "That's not necessary. I can take a cab."

"And how are you going to pay for a cab?"

She swallowed a sigh. He was right again. As long as she had no money or ID, she was entirely at his mercy. She hadn't liked the feeling before, and she certainly didn't like it now that she was wide awake and thinking clearly. "If you could loan me cab fare, I promise to repay you as soon as I can."

"Or you can save your money and I can give you a ride."

It was a perfectly sensible suggestion. She still resisted

it with everything she had. She needed to extricate herself from this man as quickly as possible before she fell even more into his debt.

She could have Karen pick her up, but there was the chance someone might follow her here. Anyone would know Karen was the person she would most likely contact if she needed help. It would only make sense that they'd be watching her to see if Karen could lead them to her. Her original plan had been to meet Karen in a public place. It was still the most sensible course of action.

"Look, I've taken up enough of your time. I'm sure you have to go to work or something."

"Not an issue," he said with a casualness that rang false. "I'm on a leave of absence at the moment."

She didn't miss how he looked away, or the sudden tension that gripped his features. "I'm guessing not by your own choice."

He hesitated a long moment before admitting, with a touch of sheepishness, "I punched a patient's husband."

She shouldn't have been surprised. She knew he was capable of anger. The way he'd argued with the doctor from Thornwood who'd called him last night had certainly told her that much. And there was no denying he had the physical strength. But for some reason she couldn't picture this man, with his gentle hands and open smile, punching someone like that.

"What happened?" she asked, curious in spite of herself.

"It doesn't matter. You have more important things to worry about than my troubles."

"Maybe, but I wouldn't have asked if I wasn't interested."

He appeared to consider this, and, unable to impeach her logic, sighed. "It was last month. I was already having a lousy day, one of those where it seems like nothing goes right and each patient is in worse shape than the last. We had this family come in from a car accident. Two parents, three kids. I spent an hour working on one of them, this five-year-old boy I almost thought was going to make it. He didn't. There were no survivors.

"And then I turned around and saw this woman waiting to be treated for a broken arm. I don't know if Beth mentioned it, but we both volunteer at a shelter downtown." Claire nodded. "Well, I remembered this woman from the shelter. A couple of times she'd managed to get up the courage to leave her husband, only to turn around and go back to him. The last time I'd seen her, she had a black eye. She didn't this time, but the look on her face was the same. She was scared. From what I knew about her, this wasn't the first time she'd suffered a broken arm—and not just that arm, either—as well as fractures to her leg, her wrist and several fingers.

"So I went over. When I asked her if her husband had done this to her, she nodded and asked me not to say anything. And then her husband showed up. I guess he'd been filling out the paperwork. He tried playing the loving husband, pretending to be so concerned and unsure how she'd hurt herself. Except I saw the exact moment when he knew I wasn't buying it, and something changed. He kept talking, but he did it with this smirk on his face. I could tell he knew that I knew, and he didn't think I could do a damn thing about it. And I snapped and did something about it. So now he's suing me."

"Did you explain why you did it?"

"Sure. Not that it mattered. It was my word against his, and he denied it, of course. And even if anyone had backed me up, it wouldn't have excused what I did."

"What did his wife say?"

His jaw tightened. "That she hurt herself. It was an accident. She's just really clumsy."

"I'm sorry."

He shook his head. "It's my fault. I can't expect her to save me from my own mistakes, especially when she needs to focus on saving herself. I shouldn't have done it. Now he's a saint and I'm an angry hothead who deserves to lose my job."

With that note of finality, he scooped the eggs onto a plate and placed it before her. She wanted to tell him that everything would work out, but she knew all too well how hollow those words would be, especially since she was still trying to convince herself that they applied to her own situation. "It sounds like you have enough to deal with without taking on my troubles."

He raised his head and looked her straight in the eye. Something in his expression sent a warning shooting up her spine. "Someone attacked Beth this morning. He had a gun and a picture of you and demanded to know where you were."

She couldn't hold back a gasp. "Is she all right?"

"She was shaken up, but she managed to fight him off and get away. From the way she described him, he's the same man I saw with the team from Thornwood who came to retrieve you. The man with the gun, no doubt the same one he used to threaten Beth last night."

Guilt washed over her. "All the more reason for you to stay out of this. I never meant to put anyone else in danger."

"All the more reason why you shouldn't be dealing with this alone," he shot back. "You need to go to the police—"

"No police," she said firmly. "I told you. Milton—"

"Then at least let me help. You don't have to do this all by yourself. These people mean business, Claire."

"You think I don't know that? They locked me up in a mental institution for four months and tried to drug me out of my mind. I never thought they were kidding around."

"So why won't you let me help you?"

"Because I don't want to put anyone else in danger. And it's not necessary. I have Karen, just as soon as I get in touch with her."

"You don't mind putting her in danger?"

"Hopefully she'll be able to provide me with some information that'll help me get to the bottom of this quickly, and then no one will be in danger."

"At least let me give you a ride to meet her." When she opened her mouth to argue further, he held up a hand. "If not for yourself, then do it for me. I'd like to know you're safe. I don't need any more regrets."

She knew he was manipulating her. She just didn't know how to turn him down when he put it that way. He'd already done more for her than she ever would have expected from anyone. Turning down his request, even if it was all about helping her and possibly endangering himself, somehow seemed wrong.

"All right. One ride." And then they would be parting company, whether he liked it or not.

Seemingly satisfied, he turned away. She let out a relieved sigh and started to dial.

She'd always had to stand on her own two feet. The only way she could reclaim everything they'd taken from her, to prove not only her right but her ability to gain control of Preston Aeronautics, was to do so again. She wasn't about to let this man, despite his best intentions, rob her of that.

The only way to ensure he didn't was to say goodbye.

"Do you see her?" Josh muttered under his breath.

"Not yet," Claire responded just as quietly.

They stood at the edge of a public park not far from Karen's apartment, partially hidden in the shadows of the trees bordering the grassy fields. They were both wearing sunglasses and baseball caps. Besides disguising their appearances somewhat, the accessories helped them fit in with the rest of the people around the park.

They'd left the car several blocks away. He could tell Claire was annoyed by his continued presence, clearly having expected him to drop her off and leave. He wasn't going anywhere until he knew exactly what was going on.

"Who is this woman again?" Josh asked, curious about this person Claire trusted enough to turn to for help.

Claire hesitated a half beat before admitting, "She's my assistant."

He felt a flash of surprise. The one person she trusted the most in the world was her assistant? Then he remembered how important her business was to her. Perhaps it made sense that she would reach out to someone involved with it.

"And you're sure you can trust her?"

"Of course," she said, as though it wasn't even an issue.

"Enough to risk being caught and sent back to Thornwood, if not worse?"

Her jaw lifted obstinately. "Yes."

The utter faith in her voice surprised him. He would have thought the idea of going back to Thornwood would make her more skeptical of anyone and everyone.

"There's Karen."

Josh followed Claire's nod to a middle-aged woman with curly brown hair who'd taken a seat on a bench. As he watched, the woman fidgeted and shot a few nervous glances around her. She seemed innocuous enough. Something about the setup still made him uneasy.

Claire seemed to agree. He might have expected her to move forward now that she'd spotted her friend. Instead, she stayed where she was, scanning the park somewhat warily.

"What is it?" he asked.

"I just want to be sure she wasn't followed."

So she'd picked up on it, too. "She does seem nervous. Do you think she sensed someone behind her on the way here?"

"I don't think clandestine meetings in the park are part of her regular routine. I'd like to think all this subterfuge just got to her."

"But you don't."

Again, she waited a long moment before answering. "I just don't know."

And wasn't sure she could take the risk, he gathered from her edginess. He didn't blame her. After everything she'd gone through to escape Thornwood, she couldn't be eager to chance having anyone catch her and send her back.

He looked again at the woman on the bench. Again, that sense of unease washed over him, the suspicion that something wasn't right about the situation.

"How about this?" he said. "Why don't you stay here? Let me talk to her. If it's safe, I'll motion for you to join us. If not, I'll hightail it out of there and we'll leave."

He expected her to agree immediately. There was no reason not to. It was a sensible course of action that would shield her from exposure.

Instead, she glanced back toward Karen, uncertainty in her eyes. No, it was more than that. There was outright nervousness in the way Claire's gaze shifted back and forth and she pursed her mouth.

She didn't want him talking to the woman alone, he realized. But why? Because she would reveal that something Claire had told him wasn't true?

"All right," she finally relented, cutting off his suspicions without vanquishing them. "But as soon as Karen confirms she wasn't followed, you'd better call me over. I need to talk to her myself."

Her words made sense, but again, something about her vehemence struck him as off. Trying not to let his misgivings show, he nodded. "Agreed."

The doubt in her face said she was still having second thoughts about this arrangement. Before she could change her mind, he gave her shoulder a gentle squeeze and moved away.

Rather than heading straight toward the woman, he took a roundabout path, venturing right at a forty-five degree angle then doubling back. As he came closer, he saw her hands weren't simply folded in her lap. She was wringing the strap of her purse. Her gaze skimmed right over him as he approached, dismissing him, but not before he saw that her face was rigid with tension.

The woman didn't look nervous. She looked guilty as hell.

An uncomfortable suspicion forming in his gut, he walked up to her and softly asked, "Karen?"

She looked up, plainly startled. He continued quickly. "I'm Josh. I'm a friend of Claire's."

She cast another anxious glance around them. "Where is Claire?"

"She's nearby." He lowered himself onto the seat next

to her. "We wanted to be sure it was safe for her to come out and meet with you. But it's not, is it, Karen?"

The flush that darkened her cheeks was his answer.

"Did you tell someone about this meeting?"

She swallowed hard. "You make it sound so sinister."

Anger spiked through him. "Isn't it? She thinks you're her friend. She asked you not to tell anyone about this meeting, and you betrayed her."

"I am her friend. And as her friend, I believe she should get the help she needs. If you were really Claire's friend, you'd understand that."

"What are you talking about?"

She leaned closer, intensity burning in both her face and her words. "She's not well. I wish that wasn't the case, but I know it better than anyone. I'm the one who first noticed when she started losing it. Of course, I was always watching for it, just in case. I never wanted it to happen, but when it did, the signs were unmistakable. I knew I had to tell someone."

She might as well have been speaking a foreign language, for all the sense she made. "What do you mean she was losing it?"

"She started zoning out. I'd come into the office and find her staring off into space with this glassy look in her eyes, and I'd have to call her name several times to get her to snap out of it. She became forgetful, missed meetings. She tried to cover it up, but I knew what was happening."

An uneasy feeling slid through him. "Drugs?"

She looked at him like he was the idiot he was starting to feel like. "No. She was losing her mind, just like her mother."

"Her mother lost her mind?"

Her eyes narrowed to slits. "Everybody knows that. She spent the last twenty years of her life in an asylum. You claim to be Claire's friend and you don't know about her mother?"

"I'm enough of a friend to know she doesn't deserve to be stashed away in a place where she's being hurt. That's not what I call help."

Karen blanched. "Mr. Preston didn't say anything about that."

"Mr. Preston? It wasn't Milton Vaughn who sent you?"

She gave him that look again that said he was an idiot. "Mr. Vaughn died four months ago. Claire's uncle Gerald took over after his death."

"This happened at the same time Claire disappeared?"

"Yes. Mr. Preston made an announcement that Claire had decided to take some time off from the company in the wake of Milton's death. I was the only one who knew the real reason why she was away, because I'm the one who told him about her behavior. But I didn't know she was hospitalized. We all thought she was in Hawaii. Until this morning."

"What happened this morning?"

"Mr. Preston called me into his office and told me that Claire had actually been institutionalized all this time. He said she'd escaped, and he thought she might try to contact me."

"And when Claire called you, he's the one you told about this meeting."

"Yes."

"And Mr. Preston sent someone with you to apprehend Claire."

"No," she said, but she sounded no more convinced of her denial than he was. Again, she glanced around, and he understood. Preston might not have sent someone to accompany her, but it was clear he'd sent someone all the same. Karen sensed it as much as Josh did.

He had to get back to Claire.

"There's just one thing I don't understand. You said Preston called you into his office. Do you still work at the company?"

"Yes."

It didn't make sense. Why would they keep someone loyal to Claire on the payroll?

The most obvious answer: they wouldn't.

"So when you noticed Claire's strange behavior, were you really looking out for her or for yourself?"

In an instant, her face hardened, twisting into something ugly. She lifted her chin and glared at him. "I've worked at the company for twenty-five years. I can't afford to have it dismantled because there's a crazy person in charge. Some of us aren't rich kids with trust funds. We need our jobs to survive."

Bitterness threaded through every word. Josh could barely keep his disgust in check. This woman was no friend of Claire's. He doubted she ever had been.

Claire was going to be crushed.

Or worse.

The reminder brought back the urgency of their current situation. Claire was in danger. He had to get her out of here.

Turning his back to the woman, he took one step toward Claire's hiding place, then stopped. A warning began to shoot along his nerve endings.

Someone was watching him. Not Claire, either. This person had no good intentions. No doubt the person Claire's uncle had sent to retrieve her.

Josh couldn't head back to Claire. He'd be leading

whoever was watching right to her. Even if he took an indirect route, he could be followed.

He started walking to his left, nowhere near Claire's direction. He hadn't quite decided what to do yet. He only knew he couldn't keep standing there, alerting the unseen watcher his presence had been noticed.

The park was fairly crowded. Children chased each other across the grass, their happy cries sounding overly shrill, scraping against his already edgy nerves. Parents watched indulgently from nearby benches, while couples lazed about on blankets and dogs chased Frisbees and balls thrown by their masters. Everything seemed so ordinary. Too ordinary. Josh had the feeling this was the calm just before something bad happens and all hell breaks loose.

Suddenly he became aware of someone coming up too close behind him. Before he could react, he felt something dig into the small of his back.

A low voice, lightly accented and thoroughly vicious, murmured in his ear.

"What you feel at your back is my weapon aimed at your spine. It is equipped with a silencer. I can kill you and walk away before anyone knows what has happened. Or perhaps I will shoot one of these children. Do you understand?"

Alarm gripped Josh's throat in a tight vise. He could handle a threat to himself, but he wasn't about to let anything happen to an innocent bystander, let alone a child.

He gave a tight nod.

"Good." The bastard drove the barrel into Josh's back, nudging him forward. "Now move."

Chapter Six

Claire watched in confusion as Josh left Karen without heading back toward where she was hiding. Instead, he drifted down the sidewalk with no apparent destination, his stride slow and easy. She glanced at Karen, who continued to sit there with an uncertain look on her face, then back to Josh. What had happened? Did he expect her to follow? If so, he hadn't given her any signal that she'd noticed.

Then he suddenly stiffened and changed course again, heading out of the park.

Even if the tautness in his face and his posture hadn't told Claire something was wrong, the sight of the man behind him would have done it. Like them, he was wearing dark glasses and a hat pulled down low. He was also standing too close to Josh, practically centimeters away, as the two of them moved toward a nearby alley. Then there was the look on his face. Cold. Intent. She'd never seen this man before in her life, but suddenly she knew. This was the man who'd attacked Beth last night. The man who'd come to Josh's house to force her back to Thornwood.

Stunned horror washed over her. She'd been right. Karen had been followed.

As she watched, Josh and the other man disappeared from sight.

Unable to remain still any longer, Claire shot into motion, heading in the direction they'd gone. She cast a glance across the crowded park. No one else seemed to have noticed anything was wrong. Even Karen continued to sit there, peering around herself with that same nervous look on her face Claire now understood.

There weren't even any police officers in view. She might not have wanted to turn to them for herself, but she would have made an exception in this case. Not that she knew what she would have told them.

No. Once again, there was no one she could count on but herself.

All too aware that precious moments were racing by, she picked up her pace. A nebulous plan began to formulate in the back of her mind. She slowed for just an instant, reaching down and grabbing a fistful of dirt, then quickly continued toward the alley where Josh and the other man had disappeared.

Approaching the entrance, she stopped at the lip of the alley, listened carefully, then peeked around the corner.

Josh and the other man had stopped halfway down the row. Their backs were to her. No one else was in sight.

"Where is she?" the stranger demanded. The cruelty in his tone sent a jolt through her. His right arm was bent at the elbow, and Claire had no doubt he was holding a gun.

Josh didn't say anything.

Her hand tightening on the dirt clutched in her fist, Claire inched forward, moving with the utmost care not to make a single sound. Broken glass glittered up at her from the pavement. She did her best to avoid it, walking on the balls of her feet.

"Answer me," the man said. From the deepening of his tone, he was rapidly losing patience, if he'd had much at all.

Still Josh said nothing.

Her heart thudding a mile a minute, she had to admire his resolve, even as she was terrified by his situation. All because of her.

They were only a few yards away. Neither man gave any impression he'd noticed they weren't alone.

The click of a gun being cocked filled the air. Claire's heart leaped into her throat.

"I will only ask one more time. Where is she?"

That was a cue if ever she'd heard one.

She lunged forward, abandoning the need for stealth. "Right here."

The man whipped his head around at the sound of her voice. She wasted no time absorbing his startled expression before hurling the dirt into his face.

With a shocked cry, he threw one hand over his face. It wasn't fast enough to keep the dirt from flying into his eyes and mouth. The muffled curses and loud coughing that suddenly filled the air confirmed it.

Josh didn't hesitate. The instant the gun shifted away from him, he lunged for the man's arm. His elbow shot back, landing in the man's gut. Almost immediately, he jerked his forearm up, catching the man in the chin.

Claire quickly ducked to the side as the weapon moved in her direction. The two men fought for the gun, exchanging blows, their limbs tangled. It was clear Josh had the upper hand, as the other man continued to cough and sputter, frantically trying to blink the soil from his eyes as he struggled to maintain control of his firearm. Josh finally managed to pry the man's fingers loose. The gun flew through the air, clattering against the pavement and then skittering away beneath a Dumpster behind her. She quickly moved between it and the two men, not about to let the gunman try to retrieve his weapon.

As though that was his intention, his bleary gaze followed his weapon. Josh didn't let the distraction go to waste. He landed a fist in the man's face. Blindsided, the attacker had no time to react. He crumpled to the pavement.

Claire barely felt the rush of relief that passed through her. She had too much adrenaline pumping through her system to simply lose her tension in an instant.

Grabbing Josh's sleeve, she pulled him around to face her. A trickle of blood dripped from the corner of his mouth and he had a few scratches on his face, but he didn't appear too badly hurt. More than anything, he looked angry. "Are you okay?"

"I'm fine," he said, glaring down at the other man. "You?"

"Fine."

Before she could get another word out, he gently took her arm and guided her toward the other end of the alley. "Come on. Let's get out of here."

She glanced back toward where his attacker lay prone on the ground. He was right. The man could awaken at any moment. They could wait to talk until they were safely out of his reach.

Her gaze fell on the Dumpster. "Should we get the gun?" The last thing she wanted was for the man to get his hands on it again.

"No time," Josh said, moving her forward. "I don't want

to have to explain if someone passes by and sees us here with a guy knocked out on the ground, do you?"

She didn't need any further encouragement as Josh propelled them back toward the street. Matching her stride to his, she hurried with him away from the scene.

AHMED CAME AWAKE WITH A START. As soon as he opened his eyes, he winced and slammed them shut again as pain shot through his skull. His eyes hurt. His face hurt. All of him hurt. He gritted his teeth against the pain, hating the feeling, hating his weakness.

Forcing it aside as best he could, he gradually pulled himself up on his elbows. He didn't even have to look to know he was alone.

They were gone.

That hurt most of all.

Doing his best to ignore the pain in his head and the continued stinging in his eyes, he quickly climbed to his feet. The humiliation of being knocked to the ground was too much to bear. At least it seemed that no one had seen.

No one except the two who'd defeated him.

Slow-burning anger curled in his gut. He'd been so close to the woman. She'd been right there. Instead of him taking her, she'd surprised him, escaped him.

It wouldn't happen again.

Striding toward the end of the alley, he touched his hand to the book tucked in his inside pocket. He hadn't made it far through the listings before the information had come that the woman was going to be in the park. There were still numerous addresses for him to follow up on.

His instinct had been correct. They hadn't gone to the police. That meant they were unlikely to now.

He would find them. Not just the woman, either.

Now he had a debt to repay the doctor, as well.

JOSH MANAGED TO PUT OFF any further discussion until they were back at their safe house. Preoccupied with watching the road behind them, as though she expected the man to catch up with them, Claire didn't seem to notice.

Josh was grateful. He wasn't looking forward to this conversation at all.

His luck ran out as soon as they made it inside the house. Claire didn't even wait until he had the door closed behind them before turning back to face him.

"I'm really sorry. I had a feeling Karen was followed, and I never should have let you put yourself in danger."

"Don't worry about it," he said shortly, moving past her into the living room off the main entryway. She should probably sit down for this. He quickly tried to come up with a way of broaching what he had to tell her. This wasn't going to be pretty.

"Are you sure you're okay?" she pressed.

"I'm fine."

The terseness of his reply seemed to draw her up short. Seeming to swallow her words, she nodded tightly. "Okay. Well, what did Karen say?"

Evidently that was how he was going to do it. With a sigh, he turned back to face her. "First of all, Milton Vaughn is dead. He died four months ago."

She blinked, the only expression of her surprise. "Then who's running the company?"

"Your uncle Gerald." Another blink. "Karen said he called her into his office this morning to tell her you escaped from Thornwood, so he knew. She also said she told him about the meeting after you called her. That's how our friend back there caught up with us."

This time she flinched, her head jerking back as though he'd struck her. A sick sensation hit him in the pit of his stomach. She blinked rapidly, and he had the awful feeling she was fighting back tears. Then she raised her chin and straightened her shoulders, a blank, unreadable expression on her face.

"Well," she said slowly, not looking directly at him. "You were right about Karen. I shouldn't have trusted her."

"I'm sorry," he said, the words feeling wholly inadequate. "I wish I'd been wrong."

She exhaled quickly, a short burst of air that might have been a snort or a sigh. "Me, too."

He'd never imagined so much sadness could be packed into two whispered words. Somehow she'd managed it. He wanted to reach out to her, to pull her close, so she wouldn't feel so alone, so he wouldn't have to see that look on her face. From the way she was holding herself, so stiff and upright, so carefully in control, he doubted she would appreciate the gesture. He stayed where he was, even though the sight of her looking like that killed him.

"Maybe there's someone else you can call," he tried, struggling for something positive to say.

"No," she said simply. "There's no one."

Disbelief swept through him. The idea that this tough, intelligent, beautiful woman didn't have more than one person in her life she could turn to, no friends she could trust, was inconceivable. No one could be that alone in the world.

But as he watched her struggle to keep her emotions in check, he could tell she believed it. And it did explain how a person could disappear without any questions being raised. She evidently had no one to raise them.

Josh would have given anything to leave her alone to gather her emotions, but he couldn't. There was more he had to know so he could begin to understand.

He tried to choose his words carefully. "She said she did it because she thought you needed to be in an institution. She thought you were losing your mind. Like your mother."

He wished he didn't have to say the words. Each one seemed to cause her physical pain. She winced as they struck home and turned her face away.

"So now you know."

"Not really. Not the whole story. Why didn't you tell me about your mother?"

"If you recall, I was trying to convince you I'm not crazy. Bringing up my family's history of mental illness didn't seem like the best way of doing that."

"So tell me now."

"Why?" she scoffed.

"Because I wouldn't have asked if I didn't care."

They were almost the same words she'd used on him. A flicker of recognition flashed across her face. Still, she didn't immediately respond. She stood there, her arms folded across her chest, her expression revealing absolutely nothing, her eyes staring blankly in front of her.

"I'm not sure where to start." Her voice sounded rough, vulnerable. She quickly cleared her throat. When she continued, her voice had regained its customary strength. "I've never talked to anyone about it before. It's the kind of thing I've tried to keep private, even though I couldn't stop the type of idle gossip that goes on behind one's back."

"I don't listen to gossip. I believe in going right to the

source. However you want to tell it, whatever you think I need to know is fine with me."

She seemed to consider his words, then drew in a breath. "I suppose it began with my parents. They hadn't known each other very long before they got married. Only a few days. It was a completely uncharacteristic move for my father. From everything I've been told about his life back then, not to mention everything I knew about him during my lifetime, he was a workaholic. He was dedicated to the company, didn't have time for anything else. Then he went to New Orleans for a convention. My mother was a singer in a club in the French Quarter. She was only twenty-two. The most beautiful woman he'd ever seen, he told me once when I was little. Remembering her, I can believe it. I always thought the same thing. He asked her out for a drink, they had a whirlwind romance, and three days later they were married. It was probably the only impulsive thing my father ever did in his life." She laughed without humor. "Given how it turned out, it's not hard to see why.

"I was born a year later. I was five years old when my mother began to fade away. She'd be talking to you one moment, and then she wouldn't be. She'd be staring off in space, smiling or frowning to herself. You'd try talking to her and she wouldn't respond, wouldn't even know you were there. Then all of a sudden, she'd snap out of it as if nothing had happened. Or she'd talk to herself, saying things that didn't make any sense. I think I was the first person who noticed, because most of the time it was just the two of us while my father was at work. I was only five years old, but I knew something was wrong. I just didn't know what to do about it.

"It was the car accident that finally alerted others to

what was happening. She was driving me home from school one day, and I guess she either faded out or saw something that wasn't there. She drove us into oncoming traffic, and we were struck by another car. Luckily, no one was seriously injured, but in the aftermath, the doctors finally noticed what was happening, that she wasn't disoriented from the crash. She was like that all the time. By then she was fading fast.

"She'd never talked much about her family, so my father hired a private investigator to look into her background, to see if something in her family history could explain what was wrong with her. What he found wasn't pretty. A long history of mental illness that went back generations. Schizophrenia. Dementia. Violent behavior. Most of the ailments predated modern psychological diagnoses, of course. Just references to how people 'weren't right in the head,' and such. Evidently my mother's family was quite infamous in the small bayou town where they'd lived for generations. The investigator got an earful. I guess she left there to try to escape her family history. Too bad you can't outrun what's inside you.

"The doctors tried various drug combinations, anything to pull her back into our reality. But it was no use. She never set foot outside a hospital again. She was…lost. She spent the last twenty years of her life in her own world. That's how I remember her. Sitting in a little room, rocking and humming to herself, having no idea who I was, not even knowing I was there."

After reciting it all in one steady stream of words, never moving an inch, Claire finally paused to take a breath. It was a sad story, one that had to bring up bad memories and strong feelings for her. There was no sign of any of that in her expression or her voice. She'd recited it plainly, without emotion, like something that had happened to someone else. That cool, blank mask he'd caught glimpses of before was in full effect.

"And you were left wondering if you were going to end up the same way," he said in the silence.

"Me and everyone else who knew. Oh, it was quite a rude awakening for the Prestons. My aunt and uncle were appalled. They'd never liked my mother to begin with. As far as they were concerned, she wasn't high-class enough to breathe the same rarefied air as them. This only confirmed everything they'd always believed about her, that she wasn't fit to be a Preston. They'd always thought she'd tainted the family bloodline. I'm sure they would have worn themselves out gloating if it weren't so embarrassing."

"What about your father?"

For just a second, pain flashed across her features. She quickly covered it. "He never said a word about it, but every once in a while I'd catch him watching me with this look in his eyes, like he was trying to figure me out, like he was wondering whether I was going to lose it right then and there. That's why I couldn't inherit control of the company until my thirty-fifth birthday. The public explanation was that it was to ensure I was ready for the responsibility, after earning my MBA and working for several years to learn all the various facets of the business. The truth was I had to prove I wasn't going to lose my mind. My father died four years ago. He left the controlling interest in Milton's hands. Milton was also the executor of his will, and it was his job to make sure I didn't lose it before I became CEO."

"Maybe your father really was just waiting until you

learned the business. He must have had some faith in you to give you the opportunity to take over one day. He could have left control to someone else in your family."

"There's only Gerald and his son, Thad. Gerald was actually the older son. My grandfather never believed he was capable of running the company, so he passed the reins to my father and left the controlling interest to him after his death. When Grandfather passed Gerald over, he started several business ventures of his own, all of which went under within their first three years. I've heard him claim it was because he wasn't as invested in them as he would have been in Preston Aeronautics. My father didn't buy that for a moment, and neither do I. Gerald wanted nothing more than to prove his father wrong and that he was a better businessman than his brother, and he failed. If he couldn't succeed with that kind of motivation, he certainly has no business taking over Preston."

"And your cousin?"

"Thad works at the company, but only because Gerald makes him. It's mostly an empty title and meaningless position, and you're more likely to find him taking a five-hour lunch than putting in time at the office. He's far more interested in his fancy sports cars and spending his trust fund than running the business, much to Gerald's dismay. His only real investment in the company are the shares Grandfather left him. He owns about five percent."

"So who would inherit if you were found unable?"

"In that case, the controlling interest would be put up for sale to the highest bidder, with Milton running the sale, and the proceeds would be held in trust for me, no doubt to pay for my care if I needed to be committed. That's how serious my father was about Gerald not taking over. Better to have the company continue as a subsidiary of someone else's business, or not at all, than to have Gerald run it into the ground. He figured that given his lack of business acumen, Gerald wouldn't have amassed the level of funds necessary to buy the controlling shares himself. He was right. Gerald has money, but he's not that rich."

That must have been what Karen meant about the company being dismantled because of her supposed mental illness. "So the only thing keeping the company from being sold is you."

"That's right. I can't let it happen."

"That's quite a burden for one person to carry, being responsible for so much."

Temper briefly broke her blank façade. "It's not a burden. It's my family's legacy, *my* legacy. The company has been in my family for generations. We used to own a single factory that manufactured canned goods up until World War Two, when the factory was converted to make airplane parts for the war effort. My grandfather saw how the company could be used to contribute to his country, and decided to dedicate the business entirely to that goal even after the war ended. That's how we became involved in the defense industry, and the foundation the company is built upon."

The fierceness in her tone, if not her expression, made it clear how much it meant to her, perhaps even above all else. It struck him that she was alone by choice, not trusting anyone to get close in case they noticed any signs of incipient mental illness before she did. Given the response of the one person she'd thought she could trust, her instincts may have otherwise been on target.

The reminder of the other woman brought back the conversation he'd had with her. "Karen said you were exhibiting some strange behavior right before you left. For Hawaii, she thought."

"Is that what they told everybody?" she said, sounding almost amused. "That makes sense. I inherited the family vacation house in Hawaii from my father. Didn't have to wait to turn thirty-five for that. I probably would have gone there if I needed to escape."

"Was she telling the truth?" he asked gently.

"You mean was I going crazy?"

"That's not what I asked."

She sighed, his sincerity piercing her sarcasm. "Yes. For several weeks before I woke up at Thornwood, I started losing time, blacking out. Once or twice I thought I heard voices. I didn't know what was happening. I knew I had to see a doctor to find out, but I was scared and not really sure I wanted to know. Then the choice was taken from me. One minute I was working late one night at the office, trying to catch up on some things, and the next I woke up at Thornwood." She took a deep breath. "You're wondering, aren't you? Whether I really did belong there?"

"No."

She finally looked at him. Her expression remained emotionless, but in her eyes there was a flare of feeling she couldn't hide, like the fear he'd seen so clearly there yesterday. This time it was hope, so vivid and longing it damn near ripped his heart to shreds.

He continued, "Had you experienced any symptoms prior to those incidents?

"No."

"Why thirty-five?"

"What do you mean?"

"You said you couldn't inherit until you were thirty-five. Why that number specifically?"

"It's past the peak age when schizophrenia usually develops in women."

"And yet six months before that birthday arrived you just happened to start experiencing blackouts after displaying no indications of mental illness prior to that?"

"So maybe he was right to wait until I turn thirty-five."

He moved closer, placing his hand on her forearm. "Or maybe someone realized time was running out and needed to make it seem like you were losing your mind before you come into your full inheritance."

"You think that's what happened?"

"I'd put money on it."

Her shoulders sagged, as though a great weight had been lifted from them. He had no trouble understanding her reaction. It was the kind of thing she might have wanted to tell herself, but wasn't sure she could believe. She wasn't exactly impartial. Of course she wouldn't have wanted to believe she was losing her mind. It made all the difference having an outside party come to the same conclusion.

She smiled up at him, with relief, with gratitude, and his heart gave a sharp tug in his chest. He'd known that what had been done to her was diabolical. He'd never imagined just how incredibly cruel it had been. Sending her to a mental institution when she was sane, knowing her family history and the fears she must have lived with her entire life, was beyond diabolical. It verged on evil.

Then her eyes widened slightly, as though just noticing how close he was. In that instant, something changed between them, a noticeable thickening of the air. There was only a small space between them, but somehow it seemed even tighter than it was, almost like their bodies were pressed together. He felt her closeness that keenly, even as part of him recognized she wasn't nearly close enough.

Her lips parted slightly, the motion drawing his attention there. All it took was a glimpse of her sweet, soft mouth to send a charge through him. She had such a great mouth, especially that bowed lower lip, practically asking to be kissed.

He only had to lean forward a few inches, maybe less, to take them with his own.

Such a short distance, such a sweet destination.

How could any man resist?

HE WAS GOING TO KISS HER.

Claire had never been so certain of anything in her entire life, just as she knew she'd never wanted anything more. His face hovered tantalizingly close, near enough that she could see the fevered intensity in his eyes as they stared, unwavering, into her own. The thin space between them crackled with tension, the same electricity she felt dancing along her skin. All he had to do was drop his head mere centimeters and his mouth would be on hers.

Her breath caught. Her heart pounded.

She waited for the inevitable. Wanting it. Needing it.

And then he pulled away.

She blinked, momentarily disoriented, as though woken from a dream. He'd broken the moment so abruptly she almost felt like she had whiplash. Her head even bobbled slightly as she struggled to regain her bearings.

Josh took a step back, lowering his head and burying his hands in his pockets. She saw his chest heave as he exhaled sharply.

She somehow managed to find her voice. "What's wrong?"

"Nothing."

"You were going to kiss me. What changed your mind?"

"I don't think it's a good idea."

"Why not?"

"Less than twenty-four hours ago, you were drugged and in a mental hospital. I'm not going to take advantage of you, especially when you may not be thinking clearly."

His words sent a chill through her body, eradicating the delicious warmth his closeness had inspired and leaving her utterly cold. "Why are you really helping me?" she demanded, her voice as cool as she suddenly felt.

He jerked his head up, confusion darkening his face. "What do you mean?"

"It's a pretty clear-cut question. And don't say it's because of what happened to Beth, because you were helping me before she was attacked. If it's because you still have doubts about my sanity and think I need to be looked after until you've made up your mind, then forget it. I don't need a babysitter. If it's because you think I might need help handling the withdrawal from whatever drugs they had me on, then you're wrong. I told you before I don't want you to be my doctor. And if it's because you feel sorry for me, then you can walk away right now. I don't want your pity."

"Good, because you don't have it. I'm not helping you for any of those reasons."

"Then why?"

"I'm helping you because I know what it's like to be scared and alone."

Staring into that strong, confident face, Claire couldn't

hold back a snicker of derision. "Making up a story to fake empathy with the patient? Tell me you're not one of *those* doctors."

"It's the truth."

"I've been to your house, remember? I've seen all the pictures of you with your family and friends. You'll have to forgive me if I have a hard time believing you've ever really known what it's like to be scared and alone."

"And the first time I saw you it appeared you were catatonic. You should know better than anyone that things aren't always what they seem."

"So, what are you telling me? That there's someone dark and brooding beneath the confident exterior and easy smile?"

His lips quirked briefly in a shadow of that smile. "Trust me, it's not always so easy."

There was something so sadly matter-of-fact about the comment that it drew her up short and forced her to take a harder look at the man before her. She peered deep into those eyes, and for the first time, she saw the shadows darkening them, a bleakness that shook her to the core.

"When I was eight years old, my parents were murdered."

Horror washed over her. She flashed back to the pictures she'd seen of a full-grown Josh posing with an older couple. "I'm sorry. From the photographs at your house, I thought—"

"The people in the pictures are my adoptive parents, Cal and Joy Bennett. It's okay. Most of the time I think of them as my real parents, because they were in every way that matters. They never made me feel like I was anyone but their own son. I'm happy to report they are both alive and well and happily retired in Arizona. I meant my biological parents. They were murdered." He drew in a sharp breath. "I'm sorry. I haven't told anybody about this in a long time."

"It's okay. You don't have to—"

"No." He gave a tight shake of his head. "You wanted to know, and maybe you should. Besides my parents, I had four brothers. After our parents died, we were separated, all sent to different foster homes. I went from having this big family and all these people who loved me to no one at all. For the first couple years until I landed with my parents, I was bounced around, not really fitting in anywhere. I was scared and lonely and I would have given anything to feel like somebody really cared about me. So you see, I really do know what it's like."

"I'm sorry. I shouldn't have assumed. You just seem so well-adjusted, I never would have guessed you'd been through something like that."

"Yeah, well, I was lucky. I figured out early on that orphans and foster kids are a lot like puppies to some people. They only want to adopt the cute, happy ones. Those first few years, I was pretty quiet and withdrawn, which was more than some people wanted to deal with. That's why I kept being moved around. So finally I realized that the happy kids were the ones people wanted to keep around, and I needed to start smiling whether I felt like it or not. And I was right. I started to act happier, my parents found me, and they adopted me. And then I really did have a reason to smile."

He did smile at that, but the beaming face she saw wasn't the man in front of her. An image rose in her mind, so vivid she might have sworn she'd seen it in person, of the little boy this man had been. Sad. Scared. Yet smiling as hard as he could so that somebody would love him.

The very idea of it made her heart ache for him. Suddenly all those happy photographs on the walls of his house took on another, more poignant meaning. Having lost one family, he'd made himself a new one, surrounding himself with friends and loved ones. And yet, among all those people, she wondered how many of them truly knew him.

Because as she stared into those deep blue eyes so dark with shadows they seemed to contain nothing else, she realized he'd never really stopped. He used that smile to keep the world at arm's length. She hadn't made a mistake. She'd made exactly the assumption he'd wanted her and the rest of the world to make. It was human nature to wonder what was wrong with an unhappy person. Few looked twice at a smiling visage and wondered what was behind that happy façade. She would have bet anything most people never saw past his big, brawny body and blond, all-American good looks and, just like when he was a little boy, she doubted he wanted them to. It occurred to her that, for all the family and friends she'd envied him having, deep down he might just be as alone in the world as she was.

Those children Beth had mentioned, who responded to him so keenly. Was it because he was strong and kind, or because they recognized themselves in him and knew he understood some small part of what they were going through?

"What about your brothers? Did you ever find them again?"

"Gideon, the oldest, tracked me down a few years ago. I hear from him every once in a while. He's not much of a talker, but he fell for this woman a while back. I'm pretty sure she makes him write. He found the others, too. Jake plays pro football, Luke's a lawyer. I'm not sure about Sam. It sounded like he was kind of drifting, not doing anything in particular. None of them were really interested in any big reunions." He gave a careless shrug. "It's been a long time. They have lives of their own, families of their own now, I'm sure. No use digging into the past, I guess."

And so, all these years later, his family remained broken. He gave a helpless little smile she didn't buy for a second. As she watched, it was like a mask fell in place over his features. She knew that look well. She had it down to a T. She was comfortable seeing it staring back at her in the mirror. It seemed terribly wrong on him.

"Now then," he said, the change in his tone indicating a switch in both mood and topic. Even if she hadn't known better, her ear had no trouble detecting the note of falseness. "Does that answer your question? Because we can sit here talking all day or we can get back to figuring out who's responsible for sticking you in Thornwood."

"Right," she said, not fooled the slightest that he didn't want to get off the topic of his past as much as return to the mystery of her present. Even so, he was correct. There was too much at stake for them to give in to distractions. "Was the man who attacked you the same one you saw last night at your house?"

"Yes. And probably the same one who attacked Beth."

"Well, if Gerald is in league with the man trying to take me back to Thornwood, then logically he was probably involved with sending me there in the first place. Except that doesn't make sense. The last thing Gerald would want to do is make me look mentally ill. It would just result in him losing any chance of getting his hands on the company. Milton was the only person who would have benefited from me being declared incompetent before my birthday. He could have found some way to continue as CEO, or manipulated the sale so that he would profit financially. That's why I thought he had to be responsible."

"Except that Milton is dead."

"I wonder when it happened. He was still alive before I ended up at Thornwood."

"We can find an Internet café, try to find out more. Karen said it happened right around the same time you disappeared. Vaughn died, and Gerald made an announcement that you had decided to take some time off, supposedly to process things."

"And people believed that." She shook her head. "Gerald didn't waste any time, did he? So it has to be Gerald. I just don't understand why he'd want to make me look crazy when it could mean losing the company if anyone found out."

"Maybe it's time you confronted him."

"Gerald isn't going to admit anything outright, and I can't prove any of it. Not to mention it's Tuesday. He and Dinah usually go to their country club for dinner. I don't know how late they'll stay or when they'll be home."

"We could wait for them at their house."

"Too risky. One of their staff could notice us and call them, and then Gerald could contact the man who's after me and tell him where to find me. I don't feel like dealing with that guy again, do you?"

"Good point. So what do you want to do?"

Claire bit her lip, trying to figure out what she *could* do.

She still couldn't go to the police. The first thing they would do was investigate at Thornwood, where Emmons probably had documentation to back up her incarceration. Milton might not be around, but whoever took over legal matters after his death would still be able to make the determination she had proven unfit prior to her birthday and sell the company out from under her. She couldn't risk it.

"I need to prove that I was committed illegally," she said slowly. "Gerald obviously won't admit it. That only leaves one person who might."

"Emmons," Josh said, following her line of thought.

"I want to talk to him," she said, suddenly determined. She arched a brow. "It'll be nice to have a conversation where I don't have to worry about him pulling out a needle if he doesn't like what I'm saying."

"All right. I'm guessing you don't want to confront him at Thornwood." She shuddered at the idea. "Maybe we can find him at home. Let's see if we can track down an address." He turned and started out of the room.

She'd started to follow when Josh stopped and looked back at her, drawing her to a halt. "Oh, and by the way, when I do kiss you, it will be because the moment is right, and I know neither of us will regret it."

Having gotten the last word, he continued through the doorway.

A little thrill ran through her, shimmying up her spine. It didn't escape her notice he'd said *when,* not *if.*

Not possible, but inevitable.

An unconscious slip, perhaps. She had a feeling it was so much more, an acknowledgement by his instincts of what his brain was trying to deny. There was something real between them, and there was nothing wrong about it.

And it was only a matter of time before his brain wouldn't be able to fight it anymore, either.

A little smile teased the corners of her mouth as she followed him.

She could hardly wait.

Chapter Seven

"Are you sure this is the right address?"

Josh rechecked the slip of paper in his hand. "This is it. Emmons's house."

He had no trouble understanding Claire's surprise. The squat one-story structure before them was small and shabby. It was desperately in need of a fresh coat of paint, the railing leading up the front steps was rusted, and the yard looked like it hadn't been mowed in a month. Judging from how tidy the other lawns on the street were, Emmons probably wasn't too popular with his neighbors.

"Not exactly what you'd expect for a preeminent psychiatrist, is it?"

"I guess he cares as much about taking care of his house as he does about taking care of his patients," Claire said. Without further hesitation, she started up the driveway to the front door.

Josh followed close behind. They'd parked down the block to keep from alerting Emmons of their arrival. Studying the house, he wondered if they should have bothered. The driveway was empty and there weren't any windows in the garage door to let them see if a vehicle was parked inside. The curtains in the front window were closed, though a sliver of light peeked from between them. "Do you think he's home?"

"Only one way to find out."

Josh kept an eye on their surroundings as Claire knocked on the door. The neighborhood was quiet, the street empty in the early evening twilight. No one was in sight. He didn't sense any unseen observers, but there was no telling if anyone was watching them from one of the nearby houses.

"Oh."

At the sound of Claire's startled noise, Josh yanked his attention back to her, just in time to see her push the door open an inch. "What happened?"

"I tried the knob and it turned. It was unlocked."

They stared at each other for a long moment. He could tell she was as uncertain how to proceed as he was. "I have a bad feeling about this," Josh said.

"He could have just forgotten to lock it when he came home, or after he got his mail." She gestured toward the box fastened to the wall. "Or maybe he doesn't think anyone would bother breaking into a house like this."

"Maybe," he said doubtfully.

Her frown matched his. She lifted her hand and knocked again, harder this time. The force of her blows pushed the door open further, revealing a living room just as shabby as the house's exterior.

"Dr. Emmons?" she called, raising her voice slightly.

The house remained silent and still.

Josh opened his mouth to suggest they go back to the car and wait. He didn't get the chance. Claire had already stepped inside.

"What are you doing?" Josh said in a stage whisper, making no move to join her.

Her face hardened with determination. "I came here for answers, and I intend to get them. Either we'll catch him off guard now, or we can wait for him to come home. We might be able to find something anyway if we poke around."

"I thought you didn't want to talk to the police."

She blinked in confusion. "I don't."

"If we get arrested for breaking and entering, you'll have to."

"Who's going to turn us in? Emmons? If he tries, we can get out of here before they show up. And this house doesn't exactly look like it has a security system."

"One of the neighbors could see us and call it in."

"Only if you stand out there arguing with me long enough for someone to notice." With a quick jerk of her head to indicate he should follow, she turned away and advanced farther into the house.

Gritting his teeth, Josh cast another glance down the street. He hated to admit it, but she had a point. The longer he stood there in the open, the more likely it was someone would notice. And he wasn't about to abandon her. That left him with no other options.

With a muffled groan, he stepped over the threshold and closed the door behind them.

The entryway opened onto the living room and he could see clearly into the kitchen beyond. On the other side, a hallway featured a quartet of doors, three of them open. Lights appeared to be on all over the house, but he didn't hear a single sound. There was something unsettling about the silence, raising the hair at the back of his neck.

Standing in the center of the living room, Claire craned

her head and peered into the kitchen, then down the hallway. "Dr. Emmons?" she called again.

"We shouldn't be in here," Josh told her.

"You can wait in the car if you want," she said over her shoulder, bending down to examine the papers strewn on the coffee table.

He fought the urge to pick her up and carry her out of there, knowing full well she'd fight him every step of the way. It was bad enough they were in here at all, without leaving behind signs of a struggle to make it clear they had been.

Then again, Josh thought as he slowly turned and surveyed the room, it was possible no one would notice the difference. Emmons clearly wasn't married. Few women would put up with living in this mess. Takeout and pizza boxes, not to mention dirty bowls and used utensils. Stacks of sports magazines and guidebooks covering various college and professional football and basketball teams. It was like stepping back in time to his fraternity days, except there'd been an entire houseful of guys contributing to that mess.

Still on edge, Josh listened carefully for any sound to indicate someone else was there, a footstep, a muttered breath. There was nothing. The lights were on, but it really did seem that no one was home.

So what was this feeling of unease climbing the back of his neck?

Try as he might, he couldn't shake it, nor the certainty that something was very wrong here. It was the same feeling he'd had at Thornwood. Maybe Emmons brought the bad vibes home with him.

Some of the papers on the coffee table caught his eye. Curious, Josh bent to take a look without touching them. Handwritten notes carefully detailed the betting lines on every recent sporting event he could think of. Each of them had a team circled, probably the one Emmons had put his money on—if he'd put money on them. Other sheets bore complex formulas and calculations, as though he'd been trying to figure out the winners through math.

Glancing down the list of betting lines, Josh hoped Emmons had kept his money in his wallet. The football picks alone would have been enough to bankrupt most people.

Uneasiness still nagging at him, he turned toward Claire to make his pitch that they should leave one more time. She wasn't there. A quick glance revealed she wasn't anywhere in sight. She couldn't have entered the kitchen without him noticing. Moving quickly, he headed down the hallway.

He found her inside the first room he checked. It appeared to be a bedroom that had been converted into a home office. Filing cabinets lined one wall, while stacks of papers teetered on almost every available surface. Claire stood before a desk almost completely buried beneath paper, sifting through the documents.

"What are you doing?"

"Looking for answers. And I might have found some." She gestured toward several documents. "According to these bank statements, he has next to nothing in his accounts. His credit card statements, on the other hand, show the exact opposite. He's carrying balances in the tens of thousands on at least six of them. He's in debt up to his eyeballs."

Evidently Emmons hadn't kept his money in his wallet after all. "Based on what I found in the living room, my guess is Emmons is really into sports gambling."

"From the looks of these, I'm guessing he's not very good at it."

Josh moved to her side. "Which might explain why he was willing to let someone pay him to admit you to Thornwood."

"If only there was some way to prove it."

She continued through the papers. She stopped as suddenly as she'd started. Reaching up and snagging a tissue from a nearby box, she used it to slowly pull an envelope from the pile.

She stared at it for a long moment, then tilted it so he could see the logo in the upper right hand corner. "The Bright Hopes Foundation."

"What's that?"

"It's a charitable foundation Gerald's wife, Dinah, runs." Holding on to the envelope, she dug back into the papers and quickly came up with two more. Checking the postmarks, she shook her head in disgust. "Somehow I doubt it's a coincidence that the charity my aunt runs has been sending something on a monthly basis to the doctor who ran the mental health facility someone committed me to."

"There's your proof."

"Not really. This was smart of them. I'm sure the checks were made out to the hospital so she can claim they were charitable donations, even though they were sent to him directly, and there's no way to prove otherwise. No doubt any additional fees intended solely for Emmons were enclosed in cash." Still, she tucked the envelopes into the inside of her jacket and gave a quick glance around the room. "If they were this careful, I doubt we'll find anything else in here."

"Does that mean you're willing to get out of here?"

"We might as well check out the rest of the house while we're here." She turned and strode from the room, heading down the hall.

Josh briefly hung his head, giving it a quick shake, before following.

He'd barely stepped into the hallway when Claire suddenly said, "Oh, my God."

He didn't even have a chance to absorb her outburst before she stumbled backward, right into him. As soon as their bodies collided, she spun around, her hand over her mouth, turning her face into his chest. His arms went around her all on their own.

He swallowed a groan. God, she was soft. He couldn't even try to clear his head and ignore how she felt against him, because he breathed in and all he inhaled was her. Her hair. Her skin. She wasn't wearing any perfume, but her scent was still distinctive, pure woman. And just like that he was hard.

Not the time. Swallowing a groan, he did his best to move his hips back so she wouldn't notice his arousal. When all he wanted to do was pull her even tighter to him, to feel every soft, yielding inch of her against him.

"Is he dead?"

Her words, muffled against his chest, broke him out of his distracted state. At first he thought he must have misheard her. Then he remembered the reaction that had led to this moment and realized something must have caused it.

A warning screaming along his nerve endings, Josh leaned over and peered around the corner into the bedroom she'd almost entered. A light glowed within.

As the entire room came into view, he stopped short. Claire's outburst was suddenly crystal clear, along with the reason the front door was unlocked.

Emmons was home.

He was just in no condition to respond to them.

Emmons hung in the center of the room, a noose wrapped around his neck, the other end of the rope looped over an exposed beam in the ceiling. A chair had been tipped over almost directly beneath him. His body didn't even sway.

The man's head was turned toward the door, his eyes staring blankly at Josh, though it was clear he was long past seeing anything at all. His eyes were streaked with red, the blood vessels having burst from lack of oxygen. His face was blue, his tongue protruding from between gaping lips.

"He's dead," Josh confirmed gently.

"Isn't there anything you can do?"

"No. From the looks of him, he's been dead since maybe early this morning if not last night." It would be pointless to enter the room, and he didn't want to risk leaving any evidence of their presence here. It was bad enough that they were in the house at all.

"I'd like to think he felt bad about what he did to me, but I'm guessing this has more to do with all those debts. Even so, the timing is pretty suspicious."

"It could be he knew he'd be through if your story got out. Losing his livelihood would ruin any chances he had of paying off his debts, so he decided to take the easy way out."

"Maybe that's why the door was unlocked. He had to know someone would come looking for him. He made it easier for them to find him."

Josh grimaced. Emmons might have been inconsiderate enough to let someone find him like this, but he tried to soften the blow by not making it a hassle for them. Nice guy.

"Speaking of which, there's no telling when someone might come along."

"Of course. You're right." She jerked her head. "Let's get out of here."

"ARE YOU ALL RIGHT?"

Claire hadn't said anything since they'd left Emmons's house, her attention fixed on the view outside her car window. Night had quickly fallen while they were inside the house. Most of the landscape outside passed in a darkened blur.

At first she didn't respond to his softly spoken question, and Josh wondered if she'd gone into shock.

He was about to reach out and touch her when she finally turned her face toward him. Pursing her lips, she nodded tightly. "I've just never seen a dead body before."

"That's usually rough for anybody the first time."

"Just as long as it's my last time." She shivered, her eyes drifting shut for a brief moment. He had no trouble understanding her reaction. Emmons certainly wasn't the first dead body he'd seen, but coming across him like that had packed an unpleasant charge all its own.

Claire shook her head. "The worst part is, I know I should be sad that a man is dead, but more than anything, I'm just angry. The whole time I was in Thornwood, I would think about how he wasn't going to get away with keeping me there and drugging me. I was going to escape and make sure that he was punished. And now that's not going to happen. That seems like a strange thing to say, since death is pretty much as severe as punishments get. But even if the truth about him comes out, he'll never know it. He got to take the easy way out, while I'm left trying to put my life back together. He stole four months of my life and, even after I managed to get away, he stole one more thing from me."

"You can still see that the people who paid him are punished."

"Yeah. Gerald and Dinah. My family." She exhaled sharply, the sound eloquently conveying a world of disgust. "I never fooled myself into thinking for a minute they were the kind of family who cared about me one bit, but I never thought they hated me enough to do something like this. Guess you really do learn something new every day."

She lapsed into silence once more, her gaze growing distant. Josh studied her out of the corner of his eye. Her face was fixed in that cool, emotionless mask she slipped on so easily, but she couldn't keep her feelings from showing in her eyes.

She looked lost. Alone.

His gut twisted. He'd told her the truth before, one he'd never shared with anyone else. He knew the feeling well.

No doubt it was one thing to suspect her family had committed her against her will. It was another to know it.

The fingers of his free hand, resting on the panel between them, flexed instinctively. He closed them into a fist, resisting the impulse to put his hand over hers. He shouldn't do it, shouldn't take advantage of her vulnerable state by getting too close. No matter how much he wanted to take her hand, to pull over and take her in his arms, for reasons that were only partly about offering her comfort.

He wanted to touch her, period. Hell, he wanted to do more than that.

The memory of how she felt pressed up against him burned through him. He felt a twitch in his groin.

Guilt replaced the baser emotions churning in him. He

was a bastard to be thinking about her like that when she was dealing with so much.

But damned if he could drive the thoughts out of his mind entirely.

Placing both hands on the wheel, he clenched it, then eased up when he thought he felt the metal give in his grip. He doubted Mick would appreciate coming back to find his steering wheel bent because Josh couldn't keep his damn hormones under control.

He cleared his throat, trying to do the same with his head. "Are you sure you don't want to confront them tonight?"

"Better to do it in the morning when we know they'll be there. Gerald usually gets to the office by nine. If we get to the house before seven, we should find them both there and surprise them."

"Sounds like a plan."

Claire nodded. He might have detected a slight easing of the tension gripping her body. She was so hard to read it was difficult to tell.

They'd made it back to Mick and Amy's neighborhood. The street was quiet and still in the nighttime darkness.

Arriving at the house, Josh started to pull into the driveway when a dark figure suddenly appeared at the corner of the structure. Caught off guard, he slammed on the brakes, impaling the figure in the headlights' glare. Obviously just as surprised, the man froze and snapped his head up, his face plainly visible in the light.

Josh stared in shock. It was the man from the alley. Josh didn't know how he'd found them, but it was clear enough he had. He'd been coming around the front from the rear of the house. He must have been checking for any signs of them. Fortunately, Josh had pulled the motorcycle into the garage in the BMW's place.

"Is that who I think it is?" Claire said, her tone equally stunned.

"Yes," Josh said. Before he could consider what to do, the man quickly overcame his surprise and leaped out of the high beams, disappearing into the darkness.

But he was still out there, and now that he was no longer blinded, it wouldn't take him long to figure out it was them, if he hadn't already.

They had to get out of there.

Even before the thought fully formed, Josh stomped on the accelerator and peeled out of the driveway. He didn't waste time backing up, executing a turn that took them up onto the sidewalk for a few seconds before landing back on the street.

"No!" Claire screamed.

Josh jerked his head to her side to see the man rushing toward the vehicle, reaching for the door. Claire lunged for the lock to ensure it was fastened. At the same time, Josh slammed the gas pedal all the way to the floor. Something crashed against the passenger door, no doubt the man's hands, struggling for the handle. The car surged forward, and the man fell out of view.

Out of the corner of his eye, Josh saw Claire turn to look back. In the rearview mirror he saw the man break out into a run. His hand went into his jacket. He was going for his weapon.

Josh's pulse kicked up another notch. Just how far would the man go to stop them from getting away?

"Get down!" he yelled. Josh immediately pulled the wheel to the left, then back again, weaving the car around the lane to keep the man from having a clear shot. There was an intersection only a few yards ahead. If they could make it there and down the next street they'd be out of sight. He wouldn't be able to catch up on foot and they'd be long gone by the time he retrieved a vehicle.

Still, he braced himself for the bullets to begin flying. Would they even know? Earlier the man's weapon had been equipped with a silencer.

Josh waited for a tire to blow, for glass to shatter.

An eternity later, they reached the intersection. Josh sent them careening around the corner with a screech of the tires. Even once they'd made the turn, he didn't let off the accelerator.

Claire poked her head up from the passenger seat, her eyes automatically going to her side mirror to look behind them. Neither of them spoke for a good five minutes, until it was clear they'd lost their pursuer.

"How did he find us?" Claire finally said.

"I don't know," Josh said grimly. More important, he had no idea where they should go now.

Last night he'd told Claire that they would be safe here. The man wouldn't find them.

But he had.

If the man could find them here, he could find them anywhere.

And no place was safe.

AHMED WATCHED THE CAR disappear from view and knew there was no way he could catch it. He forced his pumping legs and racing heart to slow, breaking from an all-out run and stumbling to a stop. It was no use.

They had escaped. Again.

His breath coming in short gasps, he quickly returned his weapon to his coat pocket. He'd reacted without thinking, drawing his gun in the open where anyone could see him. No one was immediately in view, but he knew that didn't matter.

He needed to get out of here.

He quickly made his way to the vehicle he'd left parked at the curb. As he did, the memory of the woman turned back to look at him as the car sped away haunted him.

Had she been smiling? In his mind, she was, mocking his failure, smug in her victory. She thought she'd defeated him, outsmarted him. Like a stupid American woman was capable of doing either.

Rage exploded in his veins and it was all he could do not to unleash the furious scream pressing at his throat. He'd wanted to kill her before. Now it wasn't enough. He wanted so much more.

His firearm would be quick, efficient.

But the knife in his boot would be far more satisfying.

Vivid pictures filled his head of the things he'd done in the past, along with wonderful new things.

The things he could do to her.

He wanted her in pain. He wanted her to suffer. He wanted her to be the one who screamed, not with rage, but in agony.

Until she begged him to kill her.

And then he would hurt her even more.

Chapter Eight

"Here we are."

Josh pushed open the hotel room door and moved aside to let Claire enter. Stepping over the threshold, she took in the understated lighting and comfortably nondescript décor. On the surface, it was just a standard hotel room, no different from thousands of others in the city. But at the moment it also represented so much more than that.

Safety. Four solid walls and a door with locks to keep any threats securely outside.

The entire ride here she'd been plagued with the certainty that they were being followed and the man could appear at any moment, around any corner. She'd felt utterly exposed in the car, the windows suddenly seeming too big, allowing anyone to see them inside. Even when they pulled into the parking lot of the hotel, even as they'd waited in the lobby for Josh's friend who worked here to appear, even in the elevator ride up to the fifteenth floor, the sensation had dogged her.

She turned to watch Josh follow her inside and close the door, shutting out the rest of the world and all the threats that lurked there.

For the first time since they'd left their pursuer behind, Claire felt herself relax a tiny bit.

At least until Josh crossed to another door, opened it and turned on the light on the other side. Another room exactly like this one, as far as she could see. Where he intended to spend the night.

Apparently she wasn't the only one interested in the safety of four walls and a door.

"Wouldn't one room have been cheaper?" she asked, trying for a lightness she didn't feel as she pulled off her jacket and tossed it on the bed.

"Brad's not charging us. I've known him since high school. I knew he could set us up for the night."

"You really do have friends everywhere, don't you?" The going rate for these rooms had to be several hundred dollars a night, yet the man had booked them without hesitation. As much as she hated involving anyone else in her mess, she couldn't deny how fortunate they were to have Josh's contacts.

She didn't know what Josh had said to his friend, but she hadn't missed the look the man had given her. The same one Beth Lambert had last night. Sympathetic, slightly exasperated, but not surprised.

And then he'd arranged for them to have adjoining rooms, when one would have been so much simpler since he was already doing them a favor. She didn't doubt Josh had made the request, as well as making it clear who she was.

Not a woman he was with. Just one he was taking care of.

The latest of many, no doubt.

With a satisfied nod, Josh finished surveying the connected space. "Brad isn't putting my name down for the room, so there's nothing to connect us to it. No one should be able to find us here. We're safe now."

Claire ran an uneasy hand over her arms to rub off the goosebumps she could still feel on her skin. "Like we were safe at the house?"

He grimaced. "I'm sorry. I honestly didn't think he could track us there."

"I wasn't blaming you," Claire said quickly, hating for him to think that. "I shouldn't have underestimated him, either. Anyone willing to threaten you at gunpoint wasn't going to give up easily. How do you think he found us?"

"The only thing I can come up with is that he broke into my house and stole my address book. I doubt any of my friends would have given him any information."

"I'm sorry. I hate that I brought you into this. It's bad enough I have to deal with it without forcing you to, as well."

"You shouldn't have to be going through this alone."

"Well, it should be over soon. I'm tired of running from that guy. I'm tired of running, period. Tomorrow morning when I confront Gerald and Dinah, I'm telling them to call off the dogs. I'm not going back to Thornwood, no matter how many thugs they send after me."

"Do you think they'll listen?"

"They'll have to." She didn't care what it took. This whole ridiculous ordeal had gone on long enough.

With a tired sigh, she rubbed a hand over her face. With the excitement past, the adrenaline had drained from her system, leaving weariness in its wake.

She felt him come up to her before she looked up and saw him. Her skin prickled. Her insides started to hum, a nervous flutter that began in her stomach and vibrated through her body.

"You okay?" he asked.

"I'm fine," she said automatically. She opened her eyes to find he wasn't even standing very close. He'd stopped a foot away, the distance somehow both intimate and remote.

What was it about this man? She'd never responded to someone so strongly. All he had to do was come near and her insides started humming.

He was different from any man she'd ever known, from the driven business types to the arrogantly wealthy and powerful, even her distant father. Josh had the confidence without the cockiness, along with that natural warmth that wasn't entirely the result of his practiced smile. Again, she was reminded of Blake, as near a polar opposite to this man as was possible, and wondered how she'd ever thought herself drawn to someone like him. To think she'd believed herself in love with a man who made her feel nothing close to this.

She knew her reaction had to be influenced by a combination of his obvious physical appeal and the chaos in her life. She knew it, just as she knew that she didn't care. Whatever the rationale, it felt good to be around this man, with his kind eyes and wide shoulders, his big muscles and gentle hands. She needed that, especially now. To feel good. To feel safe. To forget everything else for just one moment and focus on something good.

As though reading her thoughts, he stepped back, that reserve firmly in place, and motioned to the door leading to the next room. "I should go."

"Should you?" She shouldn't be so reluctant to be alone. She was used to it. She was comfortable being alone.

She just didn't want to be now.

She wanted him to wrap her in his arms again, the way

he had at Emmons's house, when the feel of him surrounding her had blocked out everything else for a few precious moments.

Too bad he was holding himself apart from her as if she were radioactive.

"It's the right thing to do," he confirmed.

She couldn't help a rueful smile. "You're a good guy, Josh Bennett. But there is such a thing as being too noble."

"There's also such a thing as being better safe than sorry. I don't want to do anything you're going to regret."

There was something reassuring about his unwillingness. He might be a chronic rescuer of women, but at least she knew he didn't make a habit of seducing them. Unfortunately, that did nothing to help her now.

"And if I promise I won't regret it?"

"I don't think that's the kind of thing you can guarantee ahead of time."

She moved closer and placed her hand on his chest. She felt the faint shudder that quaked through him at her touch and experienced a twinge of satisfaction in response. He could try to be noble, but there was no denying his body's instinctive response. Deep down, he was still a man. He wanted her, just as much as she wanted him.

"What are you afraid would happen if you stayed?" she murmured, even as she saw his eyes drift down to her mouth. A thrill raced up her spine. "A kiss?"

"Maybe," he said, his voice thick.

"Would that be so bad?"

"It might."

"Or it might not." She leaned in, as drawn to his heat as

she wanted to draw him to her. "You know, it is my birthday, and so far it's been a lousy one. It's probably too late to salvage, but I really need something good to happen before it's over."

She saw his resolve waver. The heat in his gaze flared. And she knew she'd won.

"Far be it from me to disappoint a lady on her birthday...."

Even as he said the words, he was moving nearer. A tingle of anticipation danced along her skin, and her eyes fluttered closed with expectation and readiness.

Then it came, the brush of his lips over hers, a faint caress she felt all the way down to her toes. It wasn't enough. She wanted more. She didn't have to wait long. A heartbeat later, he came back for more, slightly longer this time, slightly deeper. She didn't know if that had been his intention all along or if he hadn't been able to resist. She didn't know and she didn't care. All she knew was that his lips were warm and firm and felt so very good.

Her mouth fell open wider in response. He reacted instantaneously, taking advantage of the movement to deepen the kiss. His lips moved against her own, growing more insistent with each stroke. She pushed her tongue out tentatively, only to meet his as it slid into her mouth. Their tongues collided, danced, intertwined, sliding over each other the same way she wanted to feel the long, hard length of his body sliding against hers.

She'd just about lost herself in the sensations of the kiss when his hands skimmed down her arms. She immediately tensed. A shudder rolled through her, the reaction too strong to control, rocking her body from head to foot. The last person who'd touched her there with any regularity was Hobbs. Even though Josh's touch was nothing like that, she couldn't help the instinctive revulsion to being touched there at all.

As soon as it happened, she wished she could take it back. Josh immediately broke the kiss. The spell was broken, the bubble popped. He must have recognized what caused her response, because he looked down to where his fingers lay on her bare skin, right on top of the bruises that seemed even more horribly apparent in the plain light of the room. He pulled his hands back as though scalded.

"Don't." Claire grabbed them before he could fully pull away, then peered up into his eyes when he raised them to hers. "I don't want to remember that. Please. Touch me. Make me forget."

A hint of desperation that she hated hearing but couldn't deny colored her words. She read the indecision in his eyes. She simply stared back, letting him read in her own eyes everything she was thinking and feeling. She wasn't going to beg. It was bad enough she'd asked in the first place.

After an eternity, he relented, his expression gentling. He reached out and cupped her arms just below the shoulders. Her eyes drifted shut again as he brushed his fingertips along her arms, trailing along her elbows down to her hands. It was the faintest of touches, but it burned through her, scorching her skin like a cleansing fire, searing away the pain and humiliation.

Then his mouth was on hers. His kiss was slower this time, but no less fierce. The tenderness in it filled her chest with a warm ache that made it feel as though her heart was throbbing heavily in her breast.

She reached up and grabbed hold of his shoulders,

bunching his shirt in her fingers and pulling him close. He was so big and solid, his body hard everywhere she touched. She basked in the feeling. This was what she needed, to forget, to lose herself in this incredible man and feel nothing but him for as long as it lasted.

Then, with depressing familiarity, it happened. An ugly thought, a whisper of doubt she couldn't quite ignore, floated through her mind, chilling her to the bone.

Was this happening? Was this even real?

All her life she'd feared that moment when she'd lose her grip on reality. She wouldn't even know when it happened, of course, that instant when she stopped experiencing the world as it was and started believing something else altogether. She would just be living her life, already living a delusion without even realizing it. It would only be later, when she looked back and realized something wasn't right, that she would know the truth, if she ever did at all.

Was this that moment?

Her heart began to pound even harder, the unsteady cadence having nothing to do with Josh's kiss or his touch. Try as she might, she couldn't push the thoughts away. What if she'd never left Thornwood? What if her imprisonment had finally broken her grip on her sanity, and her mind had conjured up this fantasy as a coping mechanism? She couldn't imagine one more perfect than this. This kiss, this man, the way he felt beneath her hands, the way his hands felt on her. So perfect.

Too perfect?

How would she even know?

She must have stiffened in his grasp or stopped responding as intently. Josh pulled away. Claire opened her eyes to find his face hovering just above hers, an unspoken question in his expression. She reflexively tightened her grip on his shoulders. He felt so solid that her doubts were instantly rendered ridiculous. Of course he was real. His heart pounded beneath her fingers, the heavy beat rattling up her arm, filling her with the pulse of him.

"What's wrong?"

She shook her head, embarrassed. "Nothing. It's silly."

"Tell me."

"I was just thinking, I really hope you're real." She winced. Spoken aloud it sounded even more absurd than it had in her head. "I'm sorry. It's just…things this good usually don't happen to me."

His expression softened. "Then I'd say it's about time they did, don't you think?"

Under the force of the warmth in his eyes, it was all she could do to give one shaky nod.

He gently pushed back a lock of hair that had fallen over her face. When he moved his hand back again, he cupped her cheek in his massive palm and brushed his thumb across her skin. Little sparks shot along her nerve endings where he touched her. The flash of awareness in his eyes revealed he felt it, too.

"Feel that? This is real."

She smiled, unable to hold back the wave of happiness that swept over her in that instant. "I'm glad."

He smiled back at her, the tenderness on his face wholly genuine.

He made no move to kiss her again, and she knew he wouldn't go any further. It didn't matter. It was enough. A moment, a memory. Something she could hold on to and know that one good thing had happened to her on this day.

He took a step back, releasing her from his hold. Her body failed to notice at first, the heat of him so firmly imprinted on her it continued to warm her.

"You should get some rest. We have an early day tomorrow."

"Does that mean I can count on you to wake me up this time?"

"I promise."

"Thank you," she said. The words came out husky, so thick with meaning she wasn't even entirely sure what she was thanking him for.

She watched him turn and walk away. He paused in the doorway for one long moment, then looked back at her. She couldn't see his eyes, but she still felt them, felt the rush of warmth wash over her once more.

Her insides hummed.

"Happy birthday, Claire," he said softly.

Then he was gone.

The feelings he'd inspired lingered much longer, as she prepared for bed and crawled beneath the covers.

And despite everything that had happened that day and the utter mess her life had become, for the first time in four months, when she finally closed her eyes, all her dreams were good ones.

Chapter Nine

Gerald and Dinah Preston's home was several significant steps up from Walter Emmons's. Not only was it located in a neighborhood that left no doubt they had money, the impressive two-story structure was practically designed to inform passersby that its inhabitants possessed both assets and status in large amounts.

"Are you sure you're ready for this?" Josh asked as they climbed the front steps.

"Believe me. I'm ready." Jaw set, Claire pushed the doorbell.

Graceful, rolling chimes resounded within. After an eternity, the door finally opened, revealing a thin woman in a maid's uniform. She blinked at them in surprise. "Miss Claire."

Claire didn't wait for her to move or invite them in before stepping inside, forcing the maid back.

"Good morning, Nancy," Claire called back over her shoulder. She strode through the foyer. Josh followed closely on her heels.

Nancy closed the door behind them. "Wait! I'll announce you!"

"No need," Claire said without breaking stride. "We can announce ourselves."

Their footsteps echoed from the marble floors to the high ceilings. A large winding staircase led up to the second level, a glass chandelier glittering above it. The house appeared as richly furnished as a museum, and just as sterile.

After passing down a long hallway, Claire led them into a small dining room. Morning sunlight spilled through windows on three sides, filling the room with brightness. An older couple seated at opposite ends of the table looked up as they entered. The man was gray-haired and distinguished looking, the grooves of his heavily-lined face worn into a heavy frown. He was dressed in a shirt and tie, the accompanying suit jacket hung on the back of his chair, holding a newspaper open in front of him. Even though it was six-thirty in the morning, the woman seated across from him was dressed to the nines, her hair coiffed and her makeup perfectly applied, as though she'd been up several hours before dawn getting ready. This had to be the infamous Gerald and Dinah.

Gerald's frown deepened into an outright scowl as they entered. One of Dinah's eyebrows arched delicately upward in an imperious motion befitting a queen. Unlike their maid, neither seemed surprised to see Claire. Or happy about it.

"Claire," Gerald said, with the same level of distaste he'd have if a spider crawled onto his plate and settled in the eggs.

"Gerald," Claire returned, her tone chilly enough to freeze the coffee in his cup. "Dinah."

The older woman's response was cut off when the maid skidded to a stop in the doorway behind Josh. "I—I'm sorry. They got past me at the door."

Dinah skewered her with a glare. "Thank you, Nancy."

Josh didn't have to turn around to imagine the maid

cowering under the force of Dinah's deadly tone. He heard her scurry away.

No one spoke until the sound was gone completely. Gerald made a great show of refolding his paper and setting it down, then glowering at Josh. "Who's this?"

"That's not important," Claire said. "This is between you and me."

"Not as long as you've brought him into private family business."

"He's a friend of mine and a doctor. That's all you need to know."

"Well, it's good to know you're receiving some medical care, since you so dramatically decided to remove yourself from the care we were paying Thornwood to provide you."

"So you admit you put me there."

"Of course I do. Given what you did to Milton, we didn't have much of a choice."

"What do you mean, 'what I did to Milton'?"

A trace of pity entered Gerald's expression. "You really don't remember, do you? I probably should have guessed as much. I wager you didn't even know what you were doing at the time."

"At what time?" Claire seethed. "What are you talking about?"

"He's talking about Milton," Dinah said bluntly. "You killed him."

Josh shot a glance at Claire. She looked as blindsided as he felt.

Dinah shook her head, her lip curling into a sneer. "I always knew you would embarrass the family, but even I never imagined the degree to which you'd accomplish it."

"That's ridiculous," Claire said. "I didn't kill him."

"You may not remember doing it, but I have no such difficulty with my memory," Gerald said. "I'm the one who found the two of you in his office that night. You, passed out with the bloody fireplace poker clutched in your hand. Milton a few feet away with the back of his head bashed in. It wasn't exactly a mystery what happened."

"So you jumped to the conclusion that I killed Milton and immediately shipped me off to an institution without even waiting to hear what I had to say?"

"What was the point in waiting? So you could deny it, the same way you'd been covering up the little blackouts you'd been having for weeks? It was obvious that was why you attacked him."

"I did no such thing, as I would have made fully clear given the opportunity."

"And even if I were foolish enough to believe you, there wasn't time to waste waiting for you to return to your right mind, if you ever did. I had to act quickly if I was to have any hope of keeping your actions from destroying the company."

"How did you even manage to cover up what happened? Who do they think killed Milton?"

"No one. They think he had an accident. We dragged the body to the bottom of a flight of stairs, then called the police. Fortunately, he continued to bleed after we moved him. From all appearances it looked like an accident. A few well-placed payments to ensure the investigation wouldn't be too thorough, and no one had to know what really happened."

Josh's skin crawled. Gerald discussed the man's death as though it were nothing more than an inconvenience to be handled, like cleaning up after a dog that left a mess on the carpet. After everything Claire suspected these two were responsible for, Josh had thought he was prepared for anything. Somehow he'd still managed to underestimate just how bad they were.

"And no one wondered that I just happened to disappear at the same time?" Claire asked.

"We told everyone that you decided you needed time to prepare to take over and you'd left for the vacation house in Hawaii."

"And let me guess. In the meantime, you just happened to move in and take control of the company."

"Someone had to."

"How convenient."

"Cleaning up after your bout of insanity was anything but convenient," Gerald huffed. "You could at least be grateful that we kept you out of jail."

"By putting me in a mental institution rather than letting me defend myself against these ridiculous allegations. Which you did for yourself to make sure you could still get your hands on the company, not for me. I assume you were intending to make this little coup d'état permanent?"

"After your birthday, a look-alike was going to 'return' from Hawaii just long enough to sign the paperwork handing the company over to me before disappearing again, this time for good."

"A look-alike? That's preposterous. Did you really think you could pull that off?"

"We've done fairly well thus far, haven't we?" Dinah snapped.

The glare Claire centered on the woman was so deadly Josh was almost surprised Dinah didn't burst into flames. "Yes, you have," she said with utter coldness. "But it's over. The two of you are done playing games with my life."

Gerald cleared his throat somewhat nervously. "What do you intend to do now?"

"I'm going to take my rightful place at the head of Preston. Then I'll deal with the two of you."

"Not so fast," Gerald said. "If you want a chance to defend yourself so badly, maybe I should go to the police with the truth about Milton's death."

"No, you won't," Claire retorted. "Because even if you want to risk me being found mentally unstable and losing my inheritance, you'll have to confess to the part you played in covering it up, which would open you up to criminal charges of your own. Obstruction? Accessory to murder? Do those sound good to you, Gerald? Not even you could be that foolish."

"You can't do this!" Gerald exploded, slamming his fist on the table. "Even if you really believe you didn't kill Milton, you cannot risk assuming control of Preston when you know that at any moment you could begin exhibiting the same signs of mental instability as your mother."

"Unlike some people, I am aware of my limitations. If I thought for a moment my mental health was compromised, I would immediately step down."

"The way you did when you began experiencing your little episodes?"

"That was a mistake," Claire admitted. "But I also wasn't in charge, with several thousand employees, shareholders and customers depending on me at that time. I know better now and will do things differently in the future if necessary."

"Claire, dear." Dinah leaned forward in her chair. Her voice dripped with unexpected sweetness, but Josh still detected the poison running through her words. "If you won't let business concerns persuade you, then consider the personal ones. The company has always been controlled by the family. It's a legacy, passed from one generation to the next."

"And my father left it to me."

"And who are you planning to leave it to someday, Claire? All you've done since you graduated from business school is work, and the hours aren't going to get any better if you take over as CEO. We all know you have no social life. Have you even dated anyone since Blake?"

Blake? Josh glanced at Claire. He wouldn't have thought it was possible, but her spine went even straighter. "That's none of your business."

"It is if you're going to deny my son his legacy for the sake of your ego. If you pass control of the company to Gerald, he can pass it to Thad, and he to his son someday. And Preston Aeronautics will continue to be run by a Preston. You have a responsibility to your family to ensure the company remains in Preston hands."

"Don't you dare talk to me about family responsibility after you had me committed against my will."

"Whether or not you believe it, we did it for your own good."

"Spare me. If you were at all concerned with my well-being, you would have put me in a better facility than Thornwood."

"Admittedly, it wasn't the best possible option, but we

obviously couldn't put you someplace where a visitor or another patient might recognize you. The point was to not let anyone know what really happened or where you were. It seemed unlikely anyone at Thornwood would recognize you."

"You really did think of everything, didn't you? Well, to answer your question, my responsibility is to our shareholders and everyone who depends on our products, to ensure that the right person is in charge. That person is not Gerald. Not to mention I haven't seen any indication Thad is at all interested in working at Preston."

"He's still a young man. He has time."

"He's pushing forty and still acts like he's sixteen. It's a little late to hope he's going to grow up at this point, isn't it?"

"The company is his birthright."

"But not mine? Well, if he decides he wants to join the company at some point, he's welcome to. As you said, it is a family business. And if he proves that he's worthy of taking over and I decide to step down myself, I'm certainly capable of handing him the reins should I choose to do so. Gerald doesn't need to be in control for that to happen. But that wouldn't help your goal of being the wife of the CEO of Preston. That's the real reason for this ploy, isn't it? The only family member you're concerned about is yourself."

Dinah lifted her nose and pointedly looked away. "I'm sure I don't know what you're talking about," she sniffed.

"I thought so," Claire said. "Now is my condo still in my name?"

"It's still there," Gerald grumbled. "We could hardly put it on the market without revealing you were never coming back."

"Good. At least that's one thing you didn't take from

me." She started to turn away, then stopped and looked back. "Oh, and one more thing. Call off your goon."

Neither appeared the slightest bit surprised by the comment. Dinah still tried. "Who?"

"The man who's been trying to track me down to take me back to Thornwood. I'm not going back, and no thug is going to force me at gunpoint."

"Don't be so dramatic, Claire. He wasn't going to force you."

"Then what was the gun for?"

"Well, of course, he's armed," Gerald blustered. "Whether or not you believe it, the rest of us do believe you're a murderer. He likely felt the need to protect himself."

"That doesn't explain why he's been running around threatening people."

"So he's a bit overzealous." Dinah shrugged elegantly. "We were all eager to find you. We didn't know what kind of trouble you were getting yourself into."

"I'm touched by your concern," Claire said dryly. "But you can stop pretending to worry about me and get back to worrying about yourselves. I trust that won't be a problem for you."

With that, she turned and swept out of the room.

Josh gave one more look to Gerald and Dinah. Both stared back at him for a beat before turning away with apparent disinterest.

He caught up with Claire in the hallway. "You okay?" he said under his breath.

"I will be as soon as we get out of here," she muttered back.

As she said it, she picked up her pace. Moving back the way they'd come in, they finally reached the foyer and stepped outside.

A shiny new Porsche sat in the driveway behind their car. A tall, lean man leaned against the passenger door. He was speaking lowly into his cell phone, so intent he didn't notice their presence until they were halfway to him.

He finally glanced up at their approach, immediately registering surprise. "Claire?"

She mustered a tight smile. "Hello, Thad. Nice car. I assume it's new?"

"Of course. I was getting bored with my old one. How much do you think Father will hate it?" From his grin, the idea hardly seemed to bother him.

"I'm sorry to disappoint you, but after our conversation, I doubt he'll even notice what you're driving."

So this was the cousin. If he really was forty, as Claire had said, then he either had a heck of a plastic surgeon or a remarkably stress-free life. The man could pass for a decade younger, maybe more.

He barely flicked a glance in Josh's direction. He snapped the phone shut and shoved it into his pocket, then folded his arms over his chest and leaned back to survey Claire. "Don't tell me you came all the way back from Hawaii just to piss off the old man." He grinned. "Not that that isn't a good reason."

"Something like that," she agreed in a noncommittal tone.

"I don't know why you wanted to come back. The sun seems to have done you good." He snapped his fingers with a sheepish grin. "Of course. What was I thinking? You came back for the party."

Josh wouldn't have thought it possible, but Claire's face hardened even further. "What party?"

"Tomorrow night. Father is announcing that you're officially turning over control of the company to him."

Josh watched the anger return to Claire's face, her cheeks spiking with color. For a second she looked on the verge of turning around and going back into the house.

"The hell I am," she muttered, causing Thad's eyebrows to shoot up. "Spread the word. The party's canceled."

Shaking her head, she swept past him to their car.

Thad watched her walk away, an unreadable expression on his face. He didn't acknowledge Josh as he moved past.

Claire was already in the car by the time Josh swung into the driver's seat. Her arms folded over her chest and her jaw tense, she practically had steam coming out of her ears. "Let's get out of here," she said tersely.

"No arguments here."

Josh started the engine and shifted into gear. As he began to pull out, the familiar sensation of being watched washed over him. He checked the rearview mirror.

Thad stood where they'd left him, facing them. He didn't move, even as they pulled out of the driveway and onto the road.

Josh glanced back one more time when they reached the end of the street.

Thad was barely visible in the mirror, but Josh could still see him there, watching them drive away.

LOST IN HER OWN THOUGHTS, Claire didn't even realize Josh had pulled off the road until the car came to a complete stop.

She peered around in confusion at the coffee shop Josh had parked in front of. "Why are we stopping?"

"You look like you could use a moment to take a breath and process everything, not to mention get something to eat."

"Why are you always trying to feed me?"

"Why are you always trying to avoid eating? You barely had anything this morning, either."

Claire opened her mouth to argue, trying to recall the food he'd placed in front of her that morning that she'd picked at. Nothing came to mind. "I have more important things to do than eat. I have to reestablish my identity. I need to contact the company attorneys and ensure that my inheritance hasn't been lost. I need to find out what's been happening at Preston over the last few months, period. There's so much that needs to be done I don't even know where to start."

"So it's probably a good idea to sit down and think about it for a second."

"Do you even know this place?"

"It's here and it's open. That's all I need to know."

With that, he climbed out of the car. With some reluctance she got out as well.

The diner was only half-full. Josh asked for a quiet booth and a hostess led them to one immediately. Claire didn't bother glancing at the menu. When their waitress arrived, Josh ordered a breakfast special. Not caring, Claire asked for the same, then focused her attention out the grease-smeared window at the street, not really seeing it.

"How are you feeling?" Josh asked, interrupting her thoughts.

"I've been better, as you can probably imagine. You were there."

"I meant physically."

"Oh. Fine, I guess. Why?"

"I noticed you still haven't shown any major symptoms of drug withdrawal, and something your uncle and aunt said made me think I might know the reason why. If they told Emmons that you had a breakdown and made him aware of your mother's history, it's possible that he really believed you were mentally ill. So when you continued to seem catatonic, they may have weaned you off the drugs, believing you really didn't need them. You said you felt their effects less and less over time."

"Well, that's one mystery down. Only about twenty more left to go." Claire gave a rueful shake of her head without looking at him. "It's funny. I thought the worst thing they could do to me was make me look crazy. And then they made me a murderer." She forced a laugh. Even to her ears it sounded flat and humorless. "I guess that's not funny at all."

"At least you're trying to find the humor in the situation."

"Too bad there isn't any." She turned and met his gaze head-on. "Do you think I did it?"

"No," he said without hesitation, his voice ringing with such conviction a burst of warmth spilled through her chest. "Do you?"

The warmth turned cold in an instant. "I don't want to. But I don't know what kind of drugs they were giving me or how I might have reacted to them. Normally I wouldn't think I was capable of killing someone, but maybe I had some kind of psychotic episode brought about by the drugs. That's possible, right?"

"Depending on the drugs, it could be."

She sensed the waitress drawing near and quickly clammed up, waiting until after the woman had set two cups of coffee on the table and moved away again before speaking. "I just feel like I'm missing something. It still doesn't make any sense that they would drug me. If I looked unstable before my birthday, they would lose out on their chance to take over the company. The only person with a motive to make me look crazy is Milton."

"So maybe he was drugging you."

She frowned. "You think so?"

"You tell me. I didn't know him. What was he like?"

The image of Milton's unsmiling visage rose in her mind. "Stern. Controlling. The company was his life. He started at Preston right out of law school as an in-house counsel and remained there for the next five decades. He never married or had a family. That's why my father put him in control. He knew Milton would put the company above everything else."

"How did he feel about you taking over?"

"He wasn't happy about it, to put it mildly. That's why I was convinced he was the one who had me institutionalized. I'm not sure if he just doubted my mental stability or whether he didn't think a woman should be running a business in the defense industry. Probably both. He'd made noises to that effect over the years. So much of our business entails dealing with government officials and the military. He was used to schmoozing with senators and generals, and he didn't think a woman could do so as effectively. Never mind the growing number of women in decision-making positions. He could have made it easier for me, introduced me to his contacts so I would be prepared to take over. I mean, he was seventy-five. He had to know he couldn't remain CEO forever, even if my father's will allowed it. But he didn't give me an inch. Just before all this started, I requested greater access to the financials to get a sense of the overall operations before I became CEO. You would have thought I'd asked him to hack off a limb and hand it to me."

"So it could be he was running out of time to ensure you wouldn't take over, and he decided to do something about it. In which case, he may have gotten what he deserved."

"You mean if I did kill him."

"Or if someone else did to keep him from revealing your supposed mental instability."

"Obviously, my money would be on Gerald. I just don't know how to go about proving any of it. That I was drugged, who was responsible, who killed Milton."

"Do you need to?"

"If I didn't kill Milton, or maybe if I did, he doesn't deserve to have the truth of his death swept under the rug like that. I may not have always agreed with him, but he was devoted to the company. He didn't have a family of his own. We were his family. We owe him something more than dragging his body to the bottom of a flight of stairs and telling everyone the clumsy old man fell."

"No offense, but from what I've seen, that is how your family treats its own."

"That may be true for Gerald and Dinah, but it's not for me."

"Even if he was drugging you?"

"Even then," she said without hesitation.

He smiled slightly, and she thought she saw something strangely like approval in his eyes. "I thought you didn't want the police or the press finding out about any of this. There's probably no way you can reveal the truth about Milton's death without having everything else come out."

Claire grimaced. “I know. And it’s a good thing I didn’t go to the police from the start. If I had, Gerald and Dinah would have turned around and claimed that I killed Milton, and I have no way to prove I didn’t. I’ll bet anything that Gerald is holding on to a bloody fireplace poker with my fingerprints on it as insurance.”

“So what do you want to do?”

“I don’t know what to do about Milton, but I do know what I have to do about the company. I need to find out who’s handling my father’s will, since Milton is dead, and ensure the controlling shares are transferred to me. I should have asked Gerald and Dinah what they’d done with my purse so I could get my ID, but I was so furious I wasn’t thinking straight.”

“Do you want to go back?”

“No. I want to go home. I have copies of all my important documents in a hidden safe in my condo. That should help me reestablish my identity.”

The waitress returned and set two plates in front of them.

“But first, we eat,” Josh said.

She started to protest. Now that she had a plan she wanted to put it into action without delay. It finally felt like she was getting somewhere.

Then the smell of the food hit her nostrils, and her stomach gave an eager rumble.

Swallowing her objections, she picked up her fork. Maybe eating wasn’t such a bad idea. She had a fight on her hands, and she needed her strength.

This was one fight she intended to win.

“I’M GOING TO USE the restroom,” Claire said a half hour later after the waitress took their empty plates away.

Josh pushed himself up from his seat as she did the same. "I'll pay the check and meet you up front."

She felt another twinge of discomfort as she watched him move toward the front counter. He was still paying for everything. Well, at least this was the last time. Soon she'd have her own money, her own belongings, again. She wouldn't have to rely on him for every little thing anymore.

Or anything at all?

She knew going their separate ways was the best move for both of them. He could go back to dealing with his own problems without all the trouble she'd brought into his life. She wouldn't have to dig herself any deeper into his debt. It made sense.

Which didn't explain why the idea filled her with sadness.

Trying to shake off the feeling, she headed to the restroom in the back. After using the facilities, she washed her hands and stopped to survey herself in the mirror over the sink. For the first time in a long while, she didn't mind what she saw. The woman staring back at her didn't look scared or beaten down or trying to maintain her composure. She looked confident, driven. A woman with a sense of purpose.

She looked like Claire Preston. Finally.

With a satisfied nod to the mirror, she dried her hands and stepped out of the restroom.

She'd barely taken a step when she was jerked back. A heavy weight struck her midsection. Her body lurched backward, her feet lifted clean off the floor. The movement was so abrupt she didn't realize what was happening at first.

Then she felt something sharp against her throat.

Foul breath filled her nostrils. Her back collided with a hard, solid surface. A man's body. His arm was around her middle. And he was holding a knife to her throat.

She opened her mouth to scream.

"Do not make a sound," a voice she recognized all too well said in her ear. "You will be dead and I will be gone before you can make another."

As though to emphasize the point, he tightened the knife against her throat. The blade dug into her skin, not deep enough to break it, but enough that she was painfully aware of every millimeter of cold metal. Panic screamed in her veins. One slash of the knife. Would that be enough to kill her? Or would it simply create a gushing wound, one that would take a while to bleed out?

The short hallway by the bathrooms was empty, but the dining room was just a few yards away. How could this be happening with people so nearby?

Claire didn't have time to hope someone would enter the hallway or exit the other restroom. A thud against the door behind them told her he'd kicked it open. Its hinges squealed softly. He was holding her so tightly against him she couldn't feel her feet touch the ground. Moving silently, he walked backward, carrying her out of the diner.

Then they were in a narrow alley. A few feet later, she felt him lurch as though he'd come into contact with something. The opposite wall, she guessed. He took a few steps to the right, so they were no longer in view of anyone coming down the hallway.

Claire watched the door shut in front of her.

She was on her own. Again.

Her mind raced through her options. Stomp on his foot. Elbow him in the stomach. Both seemed too dangerous with the knife at her throat.

Even as she considered her choices, he eased his arm from her abdomen. Her feet hit the pavement. The knife didn't shift, keeping her in his hold as effectively as the imprisoning limb.

A few seconds later, the light hit something in the corner of her vision. Her eyes widened as a gun came into view in his left hand. It was fitted with a silencer. He released the safety and aimed it at the door.

"And now we wait," he murmured in her ear, eager anticipation in every word.

She had no trouble understanding the implications of his actions. Josh was at the front of the diner, so he would know that she hadn't exited that way. If he came to investigate the restroom and found she wasn't there, there was only one logical place for him to look for her.

He'd go out the door, not knowing what waited behind it, out of sight.

And walk straight into a trap.

Fresh terror, more potent than when she'd thought she alone was in danger, ripped through her.

Her pursuer was going to shoot Josh. She knew instinctively he intended to shoot to kill. There was no other reason to shoot him at all. He could have forced her to go with him before Josh even knew she was gone.

But if she disappeared, Josh would finally go to the police and raise questions about her whereabouts. She couldn't quietly disappear into some mental facility under an assumed name.

If he died, on the other hand, there would be no one to raise those questions. She would never be heard from again and no one would be the wiser. The only other person who knew about her was Beth, and she didn't even know her last name.

But why bother with the knife? He could have used the

gun to force her to come with him. Even now he could be using it to hold her until Josh came. Unless he wanted to have some way of keeping her under control while he used the gun on Josh.

Or he had other plans for the knife.

Comprehension exploded in her synapses. He wasn't trying to force her back to Thornwood.

He was trying to kill her.

No, he was trying to kill both of them. He only intended to use the gun on Josh.

A shudder rolled through her as she imagined what he must have in mind for her with the knife.

"Claire?"

Josh's voice came faintly through the door. Claire tensed. Behind her, she felt her captor do the same.

Her only chance would be when he went to pull the trigger. With his attention focused on the gun, he might be less vigilant with his other hand, especially if he wasn't ambidextrous and was accustomed to using one hand more than the other.

It wasn't much of a chance, but it was all she had and she was going to take it. For both their sakes.

She heard the door opening.

She watched her captor's finger tighten on the trigger.

The blade eased far enough from her throat that she couldn't feel it pressed against her skin anymore.

She didn't let herself think how close it still had to be. In one fast, fluid motion, she reached up with both hands, grabbed the arm holding the knife, and shoved it up and away from her. From his lack of immediate resistance, she'd caught him off guard. He quickly reacted, trying to bring the arm back down. He was too late. She ducked under the knife and out of his grasp, thrusting his arm back over her head as she jumped forward. She whirled around to see his other arm moving to loop around her abdomen and recapture her. She was already out of reach, her shove having caused him to stumble backward a step even as she moved forward.

More important, the gun moved away from the door, just as Josh stepped into the alley.

"Josh, get back!" she screamed.

"What are you—" It was too late. Not understanding, he'd already moved toward her. She knew the instant he registered her warning, whipping his head around to see the other man standing behind him. The gunman's lips curled back, baring his teeth in a furious sneer. Rage unlike anything she'd ever seen glowed in his eyes.

He was far enough away that they had no chance of lunging for the weapon before he got off a shot. And with no dirt in his eyes to distract him, he wouldn't miss.

They could only run.

Josh must have realized it the same time she did. Tossing the knife behind him, the man started to switch the gun from one hand to the other. Josh didn't waste the opportunity. Ducking down, he grabbed her and pushed her ahead of him, shielding her with his body. She wanted to resist, to scream at him not to place himself in danger for her. There was no time. They scrambled toward a turn in the alley up ahead. It was only a few feet away. It might as well have been a mile. She felt the air whooshing by her. An explosion erupted against the wall. Bullets. She didn't have to hear them to know. She braced herself for the impact.

It never came. They made it to the corner. There was a sharp turn, then another, a seemingly endless maze that went on and on. They darted around one corner after another. At every turn, her heart leaped in fear that they'd find a dead end.

Then suddenly they were out of the alley. The sidewalk was less than a few feet wide. Three strides were all it took before they were out in the street. Josh fell into step beside her, an insistent hand at the small of her back. They were halfway across the lane before she realized they had moved into traffic. She automatically snapped her head to the side to check for oncoming vehicles. There was a truck and a few cars, none close enough to hit them. Not that it would have mattered. They were moving so fast they never would have been able to stop their momentum in time anyway.

They were out in the open. They should be safe now. The fact barely penetrated. She never thought to stop moving.

As soon as they safely made it across the lanes, she glanced back over her shoulder, just in time to see their pursuer burst out of the alley. Like them, he didn't miss a step, heading straight for them.

Her heart jumped. He wasn't crazy enough to attack them in the open, was he?

Even as the thought crossed her mind, he lifted the gun and aimed, a crazed look on his face, his lips curled back in a sneer that was all teeth, his attention unerringly focused on her.

Which meant he didn't see what she did.

The truck barreling down the lane he'd just stepped into.

The driver didn't even have time to honk. The vehicle hit the man dead on, knocking him into the air. The scream of the truck's brakes filled her ears.

Unable to look away from the horrible scene, Claire dug in her heels to make Josh stop. "Wait."

She didn't know whether it was her resistance or the noise, but Josh looked back, too.

Just in time to see their pursuer crash to the ground right in front of where the truck had finally stopped.

Her body immobilized with shock, Claire was frozen by the gruesome scene. Streaks of blood crisscrossed the man's face and splattered across the pavement beneath him. He didn't move. After that collision, she would have been even more surprised if he had.

The realization of the man's dire condition pierced through her shock. He could die, just like Emmons, before she had a chance to confront him, before she could find out why he'd tried to kill her.

A jolt of anger pushed her into action. She started back across the street, not about to let him die that easily. Fury clouding her vision, she barely noticed Josh fall into step beside her.

They were almost there when the driver climbed out of his truck, horror etched across his face. "Oh, my God. Where did he come from? I didn't even see him."

"I'm a doctor," Josh called out. "Do you have a phone?" The driver nodded. "Call 911."

Nodding furiously, the man retreated to his truck.

She and Josh crouched on opposite sides of the man. His eyes stared blankly up at the sky. Up close, she saw him blink slowly. He was still alive.

She leaned forward, right into his face. "Did Gerald hire you to kill me? Or Dinah?"

"Claire, I don't think he can answer you," Josh said gently.

Even as he said it, the man's eyes seemed to glaze over. After a few seconds he stopped moving entirely.

Josh pressed a hand to the man's neck. A long moment later, he looked up at her and gave his head a small shake, telling her what she already knew.

She sank back on her haunches, the wind suddenly knocked out of her, and stared at the dead man. This was the second dead body she'd seen in two days. If possible, she felt even less this time. She knew the man wouldn't have spared a moment's pity for her if he'd succeeded at his goal.

The truck driver reappeared. "They're sending an ambulance. Is he—"

"Dead," Josh said softly.

The driver's face went even whiter. "Aw, man. What was he doing running out into the road like that? Is that a gun?"

Claire lifted her head to see what the man was staring at. Sure enough, the gunman's weapon lay on the pavement a few feet away.

Her eyes met Josh's. She suddenly became aware that other cars and pedestrians were stopping around them. They seemed to surround them, a million eyes that couldn't be avoided. She realized her sudden burst of anger had caused her to forget everything else. Like how bad it would be to be connected with this. And how much she didn't want to talk to the police.

She didn't know how to begin explaining this.

For a second, she wondered if there was any way they could get out of there before the authorities arrived. It didn't seem likely. They'd already been spotted. Leaving would only make them look suspicious, and even if they did manage to get away, enough people had seen them to offer a description. Being hunted down by the police was a complication neither of them needed.

She just had to figure out what to tell them before they appeared on the scene.

"AND THEN HE CAME OUT of the alley and ran right into the street. I don't even think he saw the truck."

Detective Perry Gardner scribbled in his notebook. "And the two of you saw this from across the street?"

Josh swallowed a guilty pang. "That's right."

As soon as Gardner had arrived on the scene, Josh hadn't known whether to be relieved or wary. He'd known the man for a few years, and they were familiar enough that he figured the cop would be inclined to believe his story. But lying to someone he knew also made him feel guiltier than if he were a stranger. Not that it was a lie as much as missing large portions of the truth.

He also didn't appear to have a choice. Claire stood behind Gardner, no expression on her face. Josh could still tell she was nervous. He was starting to be able to read her better, even without the obvious cues.

She still didn't want the police involved, believing Gerald and Dinah wouldn't hesitate to bring up her supposed murder of Milton if their own actions came out. If they were going down, they would take her with them.

Her eyes held a silent plea, along with something more powerful. She trusted him. Damned if he was going to betray that trust, let alone be the one to send her to jail.

"Do you know who he was yet?" he asked Gardner.

"Nope." Gardner gave another shake of his head. "Hell, Bennett. I was wondering what you were doing with yourself while you waited for the Flynn mess to sort itself out. Should have known you'd manage to find some kind of trouble. Just can't stay away from the action, can you?"

Josh mustered a weak smile. "Something like that."

"At least that whole mess is over, huh?"

"What are you talking about?"

Gardner blanched. "You haven't heard? Aw, geez. It's been all over the news this morning. I figured someone would have called you."

"I've been out of contact. What's going on?"

"Flynn is dead."

Josh barely absorbed the news, taking no relief from it. Because the expression on Gardner's face told him that wasn't the whole story. And he realized, with a sick feeling in his gut, that he knew what the rest of it was.

"And his wife?"

"Dead, too. Flynn beat her to death before killing himself. Even though she denied he was abusing her, it seems like the incident with you brought up what everybody'd suspected for a long time. Suing you didn't bring anyone over to his side. All it did was get people talking more, and of course, the bastard blamed her for that, too. Looks like you were right."

"For all the good it did anybody," he muttered. He barely got the words out. Guilt and grief clawed up his throat, forming a hard knot, choking him. He could feel Claire watching him. He couldn't meet her eyes. He knew Gardner was saying something else. He didn't hear a word of it.

He could only stare down at his shaking hands.

Blood. He couldn't see it, but he knew it was there.

Once again, he had blood on his hands.

Chapter Ten

For the past four months, fear had been Claire's constant companion. Even when she'd tried to push it away, it had lingered there in the back of her mind, an inescapable presence.

But what she'd been feeling all this time was nothing compared to what she felt now, the dread that gripped her throat in a vise as she watched Josh.

She wasn't afraid for herself. She was afraid for him.

He hadn't said anything since they'd left the diner, not when she'd taken his keys and slipped behind the driver's seat, nor when she'd started the drive back to his house, not knowing where else to go. If she went to her place, he could try to leave, and she had the desperate feeling he shouldn't be alone.

He kept his attention on the road, even though she could tell his true thoughts were a million miles away. His eyes had a faraway sheen, his expression remained utterly blank.

When they arrived back at his house, he climbed out of the car without a glance at her, leaving her to follow. Claire almost wondered if he even remembered she was there. He walked into the living room, stopped right behind the couch, and just stood there, staring blindly at it.

She didn't know what to say, only that she had to say something. "Do you want to talk about it?"

He jerked his head up, as though finally remembering her. "Talk about what?"

"What Gardner told you. The Flynns."

"There's nothing to talk about."

"I don't believe that."

"What's the point? Talking won't change anything." He heaved a long breath. "At least it's over now."

He forced a smile, his mouth curving automatically in that practiced expression. It failed to reach his eyes, the misery there exposing it as a hollow gesture. The sight of it made her heart twist painfully.

She moved closer, reached up and pressed her hand against his cheek. "Don't. You don't have to pretend with me. You don't have to be strong."

He bowed his head and gave it a tight shake. "It's my fault."

"You can't really believe that."

"You heard Gardner. He blamed her for people talking after I hit him. She didn't want me to do anything, but like an idiot, I just had to. If I hadn't, he wouldn't have taken it out on her."

"You're not responsible for his actions. From the sound of it, he was already taking out plenty on her. This was a bad situation long before you got involved, and it wasn't going to get any better without something major changing in their relationship."

"I know. It's just—" He knocked his fist on the top of the couch. "Damn it. Why didn't she leave him?"

"Maybe she was afraid."

"I know she was. That's why she needed to leave him!"

Claire held out her hands helplessly. "For whatever

reason, she didn't believe she could. Maybe she didn't think she was strong enough. Maybe she thought he would change. I don't know. Whatever the reason, it's not your fault. You did everything you could."

He pulled away from her touch. "If that were true, she would still be alive."

"You can't save everyone."

He laughed, the sound bitter and humorless. "Believe me, I know that."

He moved away, turning his back to her. Taking a few steps, he paced a tight area on the carpet, no more than a few steps in either direction even though there was more room, like a caged animal. Trapped.

"Sometimes when a patient comes in, there's this moment right off the bat when you just know this one isn't going to make it. You ignore it and you keep going and working as long as you can, as long as there's a chance they might survive." He exhaled sharply. "They never do. I had that moment with Maggie Flynn. She didn't even have a life-threatening injury. It didn't matter. She was sitting there with a broken arm and I knew it. She wasn't going to make it." Those massive shoulders quaked once, twice. "I'm so tired of watching people die."

There was so much pain in that simple sentence Claire felt tears burn the back of her eyes. She opened her mouth to say something, anything, that would take even a bit of that pain away. Nothing came out. She didn't know what to say. Even if she did, she had the feeling it was more important to let him talk. This was the Josh he didn't let people see, the man hidden behind the easy smile. That carefully crafted façade had finally cracked. Just as she hadn't been able to stop talking after so many months of keeping silent and still, everything inside him, everything he'd been holding back for years, everything that had been wanting to come out, finally was.

After a long moment, he turned halfway toward her. He still didn't look at her. She could only see his profile.

"I found her, you know. My mother. I was the first one up that morning and I went downstairs and found her lying on the kitchen floor. She'd been stabbed. I didn't know that then. I only knew that she was covered in blood. She was still alive. She was blinking and her mouth was moving a little, but she wasn't making any sounds. And then she didn't move anymore.

"One time my oldest brother, Gideon, was messing around and sliced his hand open. He was gushing blood. My mom came running over with a towel and wrapped it around his hand and told him to keep pressure on it. I remembered that, so when I found her, I started screaming for help and I went and got a towel from the sink and tried to hold it over her stomach, to try to stop the bleeding. It didn't work. There was too much blood. When they found us, I had her blood all over my hands." He slowly turned them over in front of him to stare at his palms. "Sometimes I can still see it there, just like I see all the faces. All the patients I've lost, starting with her. I can't remember all the names, but I know their faces. And now I have one more."

He continued to stare at his hands, his eyes bleak, as though he honestly expected to see blood there. Or maybe he did. From his expression he certainly believed he was looking at something.

She couldn't take it anymore. She reached out and placed her hands over his, cutting off his view of them, forcing him to look at her. A spark, perhaps static electricity, perhaps something more, shot between their joined hands. She barely noticed it. All she saw was the look in his eyes.

It was like she was staring into his very soul, a gaping wound exposed for her to see. The pain there was devastating, so dark and vivid she felt it shred her heart and send pain flooding through her chest. A familiar feeling. Because it was more than empathy that caused her reaction. It was the flash of recognition. She knew what it was to hurt this much. It was what she'd felt in the darkest hours of the night at Thornwood when she'd allowed herself to absorb the fact that someone had locked her in that horrible place against her will. It was what she'd felt when Karen had betrayed her, when she'd realized Blake hadn't really loved her, and maybe no one ever had. It was what she'd felt every time her father had looked at her, not with concern, but with a removed reserve, and she didn't know if he really cared about her, or what her mental state might mean for the company.

And just like Josh, she knew what it felt like to push it down deep inside, which helped it hurt less at first, but so much more in the long run.

The only time she hadn't felt it was when she was with him. His strength, his mere presence, had helped lighten her load for those brief moments, and taken the hurt away. She only wished she could do the same for him.

As though reading her thoughts, his gaze raked over her face, fixing on her mouth. Dark heat burned in his eyes. Desire surged from the pit of her belly in response. That wall of nobility he'd formed against her was gone, shattered, leaving behind the primal needs of the man, no longer able to be denied. In the heartbeat before he did it, she knew he was going to kiss her, and nothing was going to stop him this time.

There was none of the gentle tentativeness of the kiss he'd given her the night before. He plunged his tongue into her mouth and devoured her. She responded in kind, the desperate need she had for him, for his touch, rushing to the surface. She grabbed hold of his head in both hands and shoved her fingers into his hair, pulling him closer, even as she pushed back with her tongue. Their mouths worked against each other, hungrily, desperately, teeth clicking, lips sucking.

The smell of him, the taste of him, filled her senses. There was no consideration of whether this was smart or right or good. There was only pain and need and desire. Though she hadn't realized it at that moment, she'd wanted this, wanted him, from the first time she'd seen him. Even more than last night, a sense of rightness, of fulfillment, burst within her, filling every part of her.

His big, wide hands smoothed down her spine until they came to the small of her back. Gripping her there, he pulled her hard against his body. Her breasts mashed against the wall of his chest. Her nipples were already sensitive, and the increased friction only pushed the ache higher. The ridge of his erection pressed against her thigh, thick and insistent, leaving no doubt how much he wanted her.

Almost as much as she wanted him. Pushing back, Claire tore at his shirt, wanting to touch the hard planes of his chest and shoulders and stomach that had been teasing her beneath his clothes all this time. She wanted to feel his hot skin against hers, beneath her fingers, beneath her mouth. The buttons finally popped free, flying loose into the air. She barely noticed, her attention fixed on the expanse of skin revealed in the open V. Her breath hitched in her throat for a moment. He was more beautiful than she'd even imagined. She lay the palms of her hands flat on his chest and ran them down his body, savoring the muscular strength beneath his fiery skin, the ridges of his stomach, the faint dusting of crisp blond hair that began at the notch in his collarbone and spread down over his pecs and belly.

Some instinctive part of her recognized that Josh was tugging her shirt over her head. She lifted her arms so he could do so. It only took a few seconds to get it off. A flick of his fingers behind her back loosened her bra. Her breasts, already heavy and aching with arousal, fell free. Seconds later, his hands were on her, the soft pads of his thumbs stroking over each round globe and erect nipple.

The multitude of sensations, his hands on her, hers on him, overwhelmed her, more than she could possibly process, all of them wonderful. She lifted her neck as he buried his face there, lapping along the exposed column with one long, smooth stroke of his tongue. Her skin was on fire everywhere he touched her, everywhere he kissed her. It was too much and yet not enough. She wanted him inside her. Now.

He must have been thinking the same thing. Their hands went to the buttons of each other's pants at the same time. He shoved his jeans down past his thighs as she struggled out of her slacks and underwear. Almost as soon as she had them off, his hands were on her hips, picking her up as though she weighed nothing and lifting her up onto the back of the couch.

He paused just long enough to tug the wallet from the back pocket of his jeans and pull a foil packet from it before tossing the billfold aside. Overly eager, his fingers fumbled with the packet. Impatient, she ripped it from his hands and tore it open with her teeth.

He would have taken it from her. She dodged his grasp, reaching down to wrap her fingers around him. His erection surged beneath her touch, hard as granite beneath the smooth skin, as she slowly rolled the condom over him. She saw him clench his teeth, the cords in his thick neck bulging with tension. He was barely holding on. A thrill of satisfaction coursed through her, knowing she was the reason. Once she had the condom on him, she couldn't resist the urge to wrap her fingers around him and stroke him just once.

She didn't get a chance to do it again. With a low growl deep in his throat, he grabbed her hips, knocking her hand loose, and drove into her in one hard thrust.

The breath burst from her lungs, even as a sense of utter rightness spread throughout her body. He withdrew, and in less than a heartbeat, he thrust again, deeper this time. Better. Then again. She wrapped her arms around him, marveling at the way their bodies fit together so perfectly.

And yet, even as she felt the pleasure roll over her skin, even as she felt the delicious pressure building low in her belly, a trace of fear slithered through the back of her mind, a warning not to give in completely. She had to hold on to one small bit of control, couldn't let go entirely. She never had. She'd enjoyed sex before, all while keeping a tiny part of herself in check, afraid that if she surrendered it she'd never be able to regain it, never be able to come back to her right mind. Even now, no matter how tempting, no matter how good it felt.

And boy, did it feel good.

He was inside her, around her, surrounding her with the taste and feel and smell of him, filling her in some way that was deeper than physical, consuming her in him. She felt that tug deep inside, hard and fierce, more insistent by the moment, pulling her toward something thrilling and terrifying, something she'd never had before.

Still she clung to that last remnant of control, with increasing desperation, as the storm built within her. It was like she was clinging to a ledge by her fingertips while a gushing torrent threatened to sweep her away. She tried to hold on as the pressure built in intensity, pushing her higher and higher, pushing her to the very limits of her control, driving away all rational thought, until she couldn't remember why she was holding on, until it was all she felt, until she couldn't bear it anymore.

She let go.

Sensation erupted in every cell of her body, a liquid rush of pure pleasure so fierce a scream tore itself from her throat. She barely felt it, didn't even hear it. She wasn't capable of caring. There was only the powerful blast of raw energy that rocketed through her, like nothing she'd ever felt before, like nothing she'd ever thought possible. She surrendered herself to it, felt it crashing through her over and over again, washing away every bone and nerve and limb of her body, leaving her feeling nothing but a liquid haze. She let it carry her away, her fear forgotten, replaced with bliss.

She could have stayed there forever. Gradually, though, she regained her senses, rising out of the heady fog that clouded her mind, back into clarity.

A small part of her felt a measure of relief. She'd let go of her fears, of her control, and come out unscathed on the other side. She was still herself, still here. The rest of her didn't care. Even if she'd lost herself forever and this moment was nothing but fantasy, it would have been worth it to experience something so powerful, so wonderful. To lose herself in him.

In the back of her mind, she registered him withdrawing. He didn't pull away though. He buried his face in her neck and slowly began to kiss his way up her neck with all the tenderness that had been missing in their frenzied joining. A new warmth began to slowly spread through her. With a moan of pleasure, she wove her fingers into his hair and pulled him to her, until they were so close if felt as if they were still joined.

And this time she held on tight, knowing that she'd found something good.

Something right.

Something that deserved to be held on to tightly and never let go.

Chapter Eleven

The first time he'd seen her, he'd thought she was almost unbelievably beautiful.

How she'd looked then was nothing compared to how she looked lying beside him in bed, the morning sunlight falling over her face.

They lay side by side, facing each other. Claire smiled, her face aglow with a lightness and joy he'd never seen there before, her skin still flush with passion. Josh could have stared at her all day, seeing her look just like this. Relaxed. Happy.

"Well, that was a nice way to wake up," she said, her voice husky.

A fierce possessiveness suddenly seized his chest. Less than three days. That was how long he'd known her. Not long enough to know anyone, really.

Long enough to know she meant more to him than any woman ever had.

Maybe he was the crazy one.

"Any regrets?" she said, when he didn't immediately say anything. He detected a hint of nervousness in the question.

He reached out and placed his hand on her bare hip.

Reassuringly, and because he needed to touch her again. "No," he said firmly. "You?"

"Not a one," she said, even though her smile was answer enough.

He smiled back, until he'd had enough of looking at her and had to taste her again, leaning forward to take her mouth with his.

He didn't know if he was crazy, but he knew he didn't care.

"ARE YOU SURE YOU WANT to get out of bed?"

Claire wasn't sure of any such thing, not when Josh was standing there on the other side of the bed, his chest bare, his hair disarmingly disheveled. He had put on his shirt and was getting ready to button it. Covering up that body seemed like a crime against nature, especially when she could be over there, running her hands over him, touching him, feeling him. Her palms practically itched with need.

Then her stomach gave an angry rumble, and she remembered just how long they'd been in bed without refueling.

She pulled a sweatshirt over her head, the brief reprieve from the sight of his body giving her time to recharge her will. "Positive. I'm starving."

He grinned at her. The memory of those lips working their way over every inch of her body burned through her. "Sure. Now you want to eat."

"What can I say? I worked up an appetite. Didn't you?"

From the look on his face, food wasn't what he was hungry for.

An answering tremor vibrated through her belly, one that had nothing to do with food, either.

There was time for that, she reminded herself. For the

first time in her life, she felt completely free and unencumbered. By the time she'd remembered everything she needed to be doing yesterday, it had been night, long after business hours, too late to accomplish anything, or so she'd told herself. Now, all of that seemed so far away. It felt like they had all the time in the world.

They'd just stepped out into the hallway when the doorbell rang. Josh frowned and started toward the door. "Who could that be?"

Apprehension washed over her. She had the sudden urge to call out and tell him not to answer the door. For a few precious hours she'd managed to forget the rest of the world and everything she'd been dealing with. If he opened the door, that reprieve would be over.

And then it was too late. He pulled the door open, and she knew her premonition had been correct.

Gardner stood there, a man and woman in matching black suits, sunglasses and somber expressions behind him.

Josh glanced from the cop to the others and back again. "Gardner? What's going on?"

Gardner's expression was hard as granite. Even from down the hall, Claire could read the anger in his eyes. "Bennett, these are Agents Lawson and Molina with the FBI. They'd like to speak with you and Claire Preston. Is she here?"

Claire felt a jolt run through her. FBI?

Josh stepped out of the doorway. "Yes. Come in."

The three visitors filed in one after the other. Each one seemed to zero in on her.

She knew she had to look unkempt and it was probably clear what they'd been doing. She resisted the urge to lift a hand to smooth her hair. Keeping her hands at her sides, she raised her chin to meet their eyes as though nothing was out of the ordinary. "I'm Claire Preston."

Josh cleared his throat. "Maybe we should take this into the living room." He motioned toward the room just off the entryway.

As soon as the agents' backs were to them, Josh's eyes met hers, a silent question in them. She lifted one shoulder to communicate she didn't have any more of an idea than he did and followed the agents into the room.

The two federal agents sat side by side on the couch. Claire and Josh took the chairs at opposite ends of the sofa. Gardner remained standing in the doorway.

The female agent Gardner had introduced as Molina opened a folder she carried in her hands. "We'd like to ask you about this man." She withdrew a photograph from her folder and placed it on the table in front of Claire. It was a full-face image, like a mugshot or a passport photo, blown up into an eight-by-ten. Claire had no trouble recognizing the man who'd been pursuing her for the past several days.

Unsure how much to reveal, Claire hedged her bets with what they likely already knew. "That's the man who was hit by the truck yesterday."

"What else do you know about him?"

"Nothing." *Nothing definite.*

Both agents studied her long enough that she suspected they knew she wasn't being entirely forthcoming. She resisted the urge to fidget, even as her skin began to tingle under the force of their scrutiny—or her guilt.

"His name is Ahmed Al-Saeed," the male agent, Lawson, finally said. "He's a Saudi national with ties to Islamic extremist terrorist organizations and an extreme hatred of the West. His last known whereabouts were in Italy last year, after which he fell off the grid. We had suspected he'd managed to enter the country illegally, but were unable to determine his whereabouts until yesterday, when he turned up dead here in Philadelphia."

When he finished his recitation, both agents appeared to wait for her to respond. Claire could barely begin to process the agent's words, let alone keep the surprise off her face. "He was a terrorist? I had no idea. Why are you telling me this?"

Molina spoke first. "Ms. Preston, you are the majority shareholder in Preston Aeronautics, is that correct?"

"Yes."

"You may be interested to know that in the last five months we've intercepted several communications that seem to indicate a connection between your company and terrorist organizations."

Whatever she'd expected them to say, that wasn't it. This time she couldn't hide her reaction. For a long moment, she could only gape at them, convinced her jaw must have fallen open. "You have to be joking."

The two agents simply stared at her. Their expressions made it clear they were deadly serious.

"What kind of connection?"

"At this time it appears financial aid may be involved. So you can understand why we'd find it interesting that you just happen to be on the scene when a known terrorist leader turned up dead here."

"Wait a minute. You think *I'm* responsible for giving money to terrorists?"

"Not necessarily," Lawson interceded, evidently playing the good cop to his partner's bad. "Al-Saeed was known to have serious issues with women, particularly Western women. Given that, it's unlikely he would have agreed to work with you, regardless of the aid you might have provided his cause."

So misogyny was her alibi. Fantastic. "But you think he was working with someone else at Preston."

"Or someones," Molina said.

"Who?"

"That's what we're trying to determine."

"I assure you I don't know anything about this. I haven't even been to work in months."

"We're aware of that," Lawson said. "We've actually been looking for you for the last several months. Your disappearance, timed so closely to the beginning of our investigation, seemed odd, to say the least. Do you mind telling us where you've been all this time? We know you weren't in Hawaii."

Whatever hope she'd maintained of keeping this mess private was apparently gone. Lying to a federal agent was a crime, not that she wasn't tempted to try for an instant. But this was too big, having moved far beyond her personal concerns.

"I've been in a mental institution. My family had me committed illegally in an attempt to wrest control of the company from me before I inherited my shares and officially took over. I escaped three days ago with Dr. Bennett's help." She nodded at Josh.

She couldn't tell what the agents were thinking, but they didn't seem surprised. "And your presence at the accident scene yesterday?"

"He'd been after me for several days, ever since I escaped from the hospital. I thought he was just a thug hired to take me back."

"Hired by whom?"

"My uncle Gerald. It seems he and my aunt Dinah were the ones who paid to have me admitted to Thornwood—that's the hospital where I was. But I don't know why they would have sent a terrorist after me."

"Your company has expanded in the last decade, has it not? Picked up several contracts related to the current war?"

Molina's tone was as dispassionate as ever. Claire still sensed disapproval in her words.

"We provide services to the military. Obviously in a time of war there's more of a demand for those services."

"It could be someone wanted to ensure there was continued demand for those services."

The certainty in the agent's voice left no doubt that was exactly what she believed. Claire's first instinct was to deny it, but even she had to admit it made a sick kind of sense.

Gerald desperately wanted control of Preston and had several failed businesses on his résumé. Just how far would he go in some twisted attempt to bolster the company's profits and make sure it remained successful?

A few months ago she might not have thought he was capable of it. After everything he'd done, she wouldn't put anything past him.

"This is unbelievable. We just found out yesterday that Gerald planned to announce he was taking over the company officially at a party tonight. Thankfully that's not going to happen now."

"Are you sure about that?" Lawson asked. "According to our sources, as of this morning, the party's still on."

Claire frowned. "But that's ridiculous. He can't—"

There was no way to finish that sentence that was true. What couldn't Gerald do at this point? Evidently he intended to continue his game plan to the bitter end, no matter how absurd, regardless of whether he could get away with it or if it made the company look ridiculous.

A sudden hopeful thought crossed her mind. "If you arrest him before tonight, though, he won't be able to go through with it."

The agents exchanged an inscrutable look. "Naturally we will want to speak with your uncle," Lawson said carefully, "but our investigation is ongoing."

Claire opened her mouth to argue the point, then slammed it shut again. She didn't have to explain the urgency of the situation to them. Al-Saeed's involvement no doubt lent greater credence to their suspicions, as well as more importance to their investigation. It was one thing to apprehend someone who was providing financial aid to terrorists. It was something else entirely to arrest someone who'd been in contact with a known terrorist secretly in the U.S. and who might be able to provide information about others operating on American soil. They had to want to catch this person as badly as she did.

But she hadn't given them anything to prove it was Gerald. No, it would be her word against his. Make that his and Dinah's. Her aunt was in on it all and would back up everything he said. They could claim Al-Saeed wasn't the man they'd sent after her. Sure, he'd shown up at the park, but there were other ways to explain that, like he'd been following Karen anyway. They could even come up with someone else to claim to be the person they'd hired to find and take her back to Thornwood, not kill her.

A sudden chill slid through her. In her shock from what the agents were telling her, she'd forgotten about Milton's death. She had no doubt that once the agents confronted them, Gerald and Dinah would play their ace, claiming she had lost her mind and couldn't be trusted, using Milton's so-called murder as proof.

Oh, God. Gerald could turn it around and say she was the one who'd been giving funds to terrorists. The agents had said it was unlikely, not impossible. She couldn't prove otherwise.

In the meantime, Gerald would announce himself as the new head of PAD. If what the agents suspected was true, then Gerald's actions had already put the company in serious jeopardy. If not, what he planned to do tonight could just as effectively kill the company, regardless of whether the truth about Al-Saeed came out.

The sudden flood of thoughts came to an abrupt end. Resolve hardened in her gut, replacing her tension with determination.

Someone had to stop him.

And she was the only one who could.

"GERALD'S STILL REFUSING to take my call."

Claire anxiously paced the enclosed space of Josh's living room, unable to keep still. From the moment Gardner and the agents had left, she'd been dialing both Gerald's home and office numbers. A call to reception at Preston had confirmed the party was continuing as scheduled that evening. Now she just needed an explanation for what he was possibly thinking going through with it.

Two hours later she had yet to receive one.

"His assistant says he's in a meeting. Nancy says Dinah is unavailable."

Josh watched her from the doorway. "Did you try Thad? He might know something."

"His assistant says he's not in the office. That one I

actually do believe." She threw a glance at the clock and blanched when she saw it was well after noon. "That's it. I can't waste any more time. There's only one thing I can do. I have to go to the party."

Josh frowned. "You can't be serious."

"Of course I am. I can't stand by and let Gerald announce to the world that I decided to turn control of the company over to him. It doesn't matter that it's not true. Perception is everything. If I come back the next day and say I did no such thing, it's just going to make us look ridiculous and leave everybody wondering if anyone rational really is in charge."

"How do you think Gerald is going to react if you suddenly show up at the party and try to stop him? Don't you realize how dangerous that could be?"

"There will be several hundred people there. He wouldn't be able to do anything to me."

Josh stalked into the room toward her. "After everything you believe he's done, do you really think he'll allow anything to stop him now that his big moment is here? If you push a desperate man, there's no telling how he'll react. For all you know, he'll have more of his terrorist buddies there waiting for you."

"I can't sit here and do nothing. I have a responsibility to the company."

"You have a responsibility to yourself to think about your own safety. You're not going to be able to do anything for the company if you're dead."

For just a moment, Claire felt the slightest bit of trepidation at his words. She didn't allow the feeling to gain traction, brushing it off as if it were nothing. She couldn't afford to give in to nervousness, to fear.

Never show weakness.

The familiar words echoed in the back of her mind, a strengthening reminder of what she had to do and how she had to be. Yet as she took in Josh's protective stance and the worried tension in his face, she suddenly realized just how deeply she'd failed to live by her own motto.

Showing weakness was all she'd done from the moment she'd met him. The only Claire Preston he'd known was this pathetic victim, a woman who'd been committed against her will, who'd been drugged into submission, who'd been conspired against by her own family, who needed him to protect her.

A woman who'd asked him to kiss her for her birthday, for God's sake. It didn't get much more pathetic than that.

Claire squared her shoulders and lifted her chin. Her victimhood stopped now. It was long past time he learned who she really was.

"Don't underestimate me," she said coolly. "I've never been the kind of person who ran and hid from any kind of obstacle, and I'm not about to start now. I don't need your approval, and I certainly didn't ask for your opinion. I'm going to the party."

His lips thinned into a mutinous line. He appeared to visibly swallow his arguments. "Fine. If it's that important to you, I'll go with you."

"No, you won't."

His brow furrowed, carving those lines she'd thought she'd never see there into his forehead. "You really want to walk in there by yourself, with no idea what you're facing?"

"I have to. Every single person there has to know that I'm strong enough to stand on my own."

"Knowing that someone has your back doesn't make you weak. Having someone care about you is a strength."

"Not if the other person cares because they don't think you can take care of yourself."

Josh's eyes narrowed and he stared at her for a long moment. "Are you worried that I think you're weak, or that you think that about yourself?"

She felt a jolt at his words. Before she could respond, he stepped forward and continued.

"Let's get one thing straight. I have never doubted how strong you are. How could I, after everything you went through at Thornwood, everything you did to escape? A weak person would have cracked long ago, and that's not you. But you don't have to be strong all the time. Isn't that what you told me last night?"

"I also told you that you can't save everybody. I'm not your mother or any other woman you think is in trouble. I'm not interested in being just another woman you feel the need to rescue."

"Is that all you think there is between us? Claire, I work in a hospital and I volunteer at a shelter. If all I was looking for was a woman to save, I could have found that a long time ago."

"And yet here we are."

"Damn it. If I wanted to save you, I'd let you throw yourself into this dangerous situation without a word just so I could rush in and come to your rescue."

His words stoked her anger. "Then it's too bad you're in no position to 'let' me do anything. The only person who determines what I do is me, and I don't need your help."

"Mine? Or anybody's?"

"That's right. I can take care of myself. I always have."

"And look how well that has turned out for you," he said. The softly spoken words were pointed, but not unkind.

They still raised all her hackles. "Regardless, I don't want you there."

"Is that why you really didn't want to go to the police? Because you think you have to be strong enough to handle things yourself?"

"I know I have to be."

"We all need somebody to turn to when we're in trouble, Claire. In case you haven't noticed, I haven't exactly been flying solo the last few days."

"Maybe you're right," she said. "I just know I don't want you to run to my rescue anymore. I need to do this."

He threw his hands up in frustration. "This is crazy."

Claire felt the words like a blow. The shock, the sting of them, knocked the air from her chest. She actually felt like she was reeling back on her heels. He couldn't have hurt her more if he'd tried. "This is?" she asked quietly. "Or I am?"

His face clouded with a combination of exasperation and regret. "You know that's not what I meant."

"Do I? Let's face it. We've only known each other for three days. That's not long enough to get to know each other. Not really. Hell, my parents' experience taught me that well enough. And you know, maybe we shouldn't."

"What are you saying?"

She knew what she had to do. The only way she could prove to the world, to herself, that she was strong enough was to say goodbye to this man and stand on her own two feet. She'd known it from the very beginning and somehow let him deter her from pulling the trigger. Even now, the very thought of it made her heart twist painfully in her chest.

But no more. This moment was long overdue.

She looked at him, her expression molded back into the mask that revealed nothing, and drank in the sight of him one last time. "Goodbye, Josh."

"Claire—"

She didn't wait to hear what he had to say. There was no point. She walked straight out the door, not taking a breath until she was clear on the other side. Even then, she didn't stop, picking up her pace before she could second-guess herself and change her mind.

It was only when she reached the end of the driveway that she realized she still didn't have any money. Maybe that was why he wasn't coming after her. He thought she would have no choice but to come back.

She would rather walk all the way home.

Then she spotted the dark sedan parked on the other side of the street, and the two figures sitting in the front seat.

Claire quickly crossed to the vehicle and tapped on the driver's window. Seeing the two men up close confirmed her impression from across the street. Dark suits, serious expressions. They were cut from the same cloth as Lawson and Molina. "Are you federal agents?"

At first she wasn't sure the driver was going to answer. Finally, he said, "Yes," his tone unrepentant, as though daring her to complain.

"Can I see some ID?"

Another moment passed before both agents reached into their jackets and showed their identification. She examined each one closely, not taking any chances. They appeared legit.

"And Lawson and Molina? Are they talking to my uncle?"

"I'm not at liberty to disclose that."

Claire moved to the back door, tried it, then tapped on the window until she heard them unlock it.

She climbed in behind the driver. He met her eyes in the rearview mirror. "Are you watching me?" she asked.

"And if we are?"

"Well, if you're going to follow me, you might as well give me a ride."

The agent in the passenger seat turned around to face her with a frown. "Everything okay?"

"Fine," she said shortly. "Can we go?"

He must have heard something in her voice. For a second, a trace of sympathy entered his eyes. Claire turned away from it and focused out the window. She didn't want his sympathy, and she didn't need it.

She'd take a ride, but that was it.

She could take care of herself.

That was how it had to be.

Chapter Twelve

Josh arrived at the party shortly before eight. Getting in without an invitation didn't prove too difficult. He'd driven by the building an hour earlier, scoping out the service entrance. The number of men in tuxedos seemed to indicate that was how the waitstaff would be dressed, just as he'd suspected. He parked where he'd seen the staff doing so and slipped into the building through the service entrance when the security guard stepped away for a brief moment.

In the frantic activity of the kitchen, he managed to melt into the crowd unnoticed. He picked up a tray of hors d'oeuvres and followed the stream of waiters into the party.

He found himself in a massive gathering hall shaped like a half circle. The party was scheduled to start at eight, and the room was already packed with people. The sounds of murmured conversations rose to the high ceilings. Like most of the Preston building, the exterior wall of the hall was constructed entirely of glass. The darkness beyond had turned the surface into a mirror, reflecting the activity inside the room.

Depositing the tray on a table with similar dishes, Josh headed into the crowd. No one gave him a second glance.

The tension in his gut eased slightly. That had been easy. Now came the hard part.

Making sure nothing happened to Claire.

It took him several minutes to spot her. She was standing a short distance away, talking to an older couple.

He couldn't keep his eyes off her, and it had nothing to do with the fact that he was there to watch out for her. She looked incredible. She was wearing a long-sleeved, dark blue dress that somehow managed to be both modest and flattering. Her hair was swept up on top of her head, a different look than he'd seen from her before, but one he couldn't argue with. Pulling her hair away from her face revealed her features more strongly, making her classic beauty stand out that much more. She seemed to be wearing much less makeup than any other woman here, and outshone them all. She might as well have been the only person in the room.

He watched as she excused herself from the couple with a gracious smile and turned to face the next person she encountered without missing a beat, immediately launching into a fresh conversation. She appeared completely at ease and in command. It was impossible to believe this woman had spent the last four months in an institution.

A strange warmth filled his chest, something that felt almost like pride. He may not have wanted her to come here, but it was clear she was in her element. This really was where she belonged, despite her family's attempts to keep her away.

At the thought of something happening to her, the tightness instantly returned to his gut. He was here for a reason. He had to remember that, couldn't let his guard down.

He made no move to approach her or alert her to his

presence. She'd made it clear she didn't want him here. He would have to be content to watch from a distance and hope she didn't notice him. She may not have wanted someone to watch her back, but she had it.

He just needed to know she was safe. As soon as the night had passed and it was clear she wasn't in danger, he would slip back out unnoticed.

With any luck, she'd never know he was here.

THE HEELS WERE GOING to be the death of her.

Keeping a smile plastered on her face, Claire slowly moved through the crowd, shaking hands and exchanging the obligatory small talk. She would have given anything to take a seat and relieve her aching arches. One thing she hadn't missed for the last several months was wearing heels. Putting them on for this event had been like rediscovering how uncomfortable shoes could be all over again.

But sitting down, even for a minute, was not an option. She had to find Gerald and speak with him before he went through with this ridiculous sideshow. Or else step to the microphone herself and make a preemptory speech of her own before he had the chance.

An elevated podium was set up in the front of the room, clearly indicating some kind of statement or presentation was scheduled to take place at some point in the evening. And hopefully unlike everyone else in the room, she knew what it was going to be.

A shudder rolled through her. Gerald really was that foolish. Or desperate, as Josh had put it.

Josh.

She felt her heart give a sharp pull in her chest. With ruthless efficiency, she pushed the very thought of him out of mind. She hadn't let herself think of him for a moment since she'd left him. She couldn't afford the distraction.

So she continued to smile and make small talk, all the while keeping an eye out. Gerald's Hawaii story seemed to have worked. No one looked at her askance, no one's comments dripped with knowing innuendo. Everyone seemed to believe she'd been exactly where her family had said she was.

As her gaze swept over the crowd, she finally spotted the face she was looking for, standing at the edge of the room toward the front, conspicuously close to the podium.

Gerald.

He appeared completely at ease. Word of her presence probably hadn't reached him yet. He still thought everything was going according to plan.

Time to give him a rude awakening.

As she watched, he moved away from the podium and headed for a door leading out of the room. The closest restrooms were in that direction, she thought, figuring his probable destination. Which meant she might be able to get him reasonably alone. Perfect.

Lowering her hand into her purse, she started to follow.

She'd just cleared most of the crowd when a hand clamped down on her wrist. "I need to talk to you."

Claire jerked her head up to find Thad had come up beside her unnoticed. She swallowed her impatience. "What is it?"

Though he had a smile on his face, he cast an uneasy glance around them as he took her arm. "Not here. In private."

He began to steer her toward a different exit from the one Gerald had used. Did he know what she planned to do? Was he trying to keep her away from his father?

Her immediate impulse was to yank her arm out of his grasp and stand her ground. Of course she could do no such thing. She couldn't afford to make a scene. From the tight grip he had on her arm, he wasn't going to let go easily. "What is this about?"

With another nervous glance, Thad leaned closer and whispered in her ear. "It's about what really happened to Milton Vaughn."

"What is it?"

"Not here," he insisted, giving her arm a gentle but insistent tug.

Claire hesitated, unsure what to do. If Thad knew something about Milton's death, she wanted to know. But her primary mission was to stop Gerald.

She glanced back toward the door Gerald had disappeared through. He had not returned and was unlikely to take the stage in the next few minutes. Maybe she could spare a minute, no more.

JOSH WATCHED AS CLAIRE made her way through the masses with Thad by her side. Unease crawled along his nerve endings. Both were smiling in that way he was beginning to be certain had to be fake, but he knew Claire well enough to read the annoyance in her eyes. Something was up.

He matched his movements to theirs. His attention was focused so thoroughly on Claire that he barely noticed anyone else around him until he collided with someone.

"I'm sorry—" The apology that rose to his lips died immediately.

Not a single muscle on Dinah Preston's perfectly applied face shifted. Evidently Claire wasn't the only one in the family who knew how to mask her feelings so thoroughly. Dinah was less adept at hiding the spark of fury that entered her eyes. Her fingers tightened like claws on the flute of champagne in her hand.

Without looking at him, she gave a subtle jerk of her head toward the perimeter of the room and slowly started away. He took that to mean she wanted him to follow her. He did so only because it was the same direction Claire had gone.

Once they stepped out of the crowd, she turned back toward the party, keeping the room in front of her. Josh did the same. "What are you doing here?" she murmured between firmly clenched teeth.

"I'm watching out for Claire," he replied in an equally low tone.

Her fingers hardened further, her knuckles turning white. He almost heard the glass crack. "I should have known she would come."

"Yes, you should have." His eyes began to seek out Claire again. "The only way to prevent it would have been to cancel the party altogether. Come to think of it, that's what you probably should have done."

"We couldn't cancel the party. There were over two hundred invitees. Even if it were feasible to contact all of them, do you have any idea how it would have looked to cancel on such short notice?"

"And it had nothing to do with Gerald's plans to announce Claire had given him control of the company?"

"Gerald can't do that. Not with Claire back to dispute it. If he announced it only to have her deny it the very next day, it would look terrible for the company."

"As bad as getting the company involved with terrorists?"

She shot a nervous glance around them. For an instant, she looked like she was going to be physically ill. "Keep your voice down," she grunted. "We did no such thing. I don't know what kind of unsavory types Claire got herself involved with, but we had nothing to do with terrorism. As we informed the federal agents who came to see Gerald and me today." Her expression turned satisfied. "Just as we informed them about what Claire did to Milton. Unlike her ridiculous claim, that one was actually true."

"Spare me, lady. How did Al-Saeed know where to find Claire in the park if Gerald didn't tell him?"

"Gerald didn't tell anyone anything," she said with barely restrained impatience. "Thad was the go-between. Obviously he didn't know who the man was when he hired him to find Claire. Or maybe this terrorist person followed the man whom Thad actually hired. That would actually make more sense."

A flicker of unease turned Josh's stomach. "Thad hired someone to find Claire?"

"Yes, just like he found that useless Dr. Emmons in the first place."

And there it was. An answer to something he hadn't quite been able to put his finger on. Until now.

We dragged the body, Gerald had said. The use of the plural subject hadn't even sunk in, since there'd been two of them sitting there, two of them involved in the scheme. Except now he realized that Gerald couldn't have been referring to himself and Dinah. He couldn't picture Dinah taking the risk of messing up her hair or getting blood on her clothes by dragging a bloody corpse around, no matter the circumstances.

No, someone else had helped Gerald. Someone he would have trusted with the news of Claire's apparent loss of sanity. Someone in the family.

Thad.

Thad, who'd acted like he thought Claire was back from Hawaii when he'd known she was never there.

Thad, who'd made sure to let her know of Gerald's plan, keeping her suspicion on his father after they'd displayed none toward him and perhaps giving Al-Saeed time to catch up with them and then follow them from the house.

Thad, whom he'd last seen talking to Claire.

Josh spun around, his eyes going to where he'd seen Claire moments ago.

She was gone.

CLAIRE WAS FULLY FED UP by the time Thad led her into the atrium almost on the other side of the building. She didn't know how much more alone they could be. They hadn't passed a single person in the abandoned corridors on the main level.

The large, airy space they'd finally arrived in was the mirror image of the one they'd just left. Only a few small lamps glowed from the floor. The glass walls gave the impression there were no walls at all and the room was filled with night, stars and velvet darkness. The only sound was the water lapping in the recessed reflecting pool in the center of the room, a feature that made this the most popular lunch spot in the building, as evidenced by the tables set up around the space.

Stepping inside before him, Claire finally tugged her arm from his grip. "All right, Thad. What is this about?"

"Tying up loose ends."

As he said the words, she sensed something rushing toward her. She instinctively jumped forward as she whirled around, just in time to see him swinging his arm down on the spot where she'd been standing seconds before. His hand contained a small gun held by the barrel. If she hadn't moved, the butt would have come down right on the back of her neck.

"What the hell are you doing?"

He simply stared at her, every trace of nervousness gone from his expression, leaving only cold purpose in its wake. As she watched, he turned the gun around and pointed it straight at her.

The horrifying truth rushed at her all at once. "It's not Gerald. It's you. You're giving money to terrorists?"

He arched a brow. "So you know about that, do you? I see I'm acting none too soon."

"But why?"

"We're in the defense industry, Claire. We wouldn't do much business if there wasn't a threat to defend against. It's simple supply-and-demand. We have the supply. I'm ensuring there's demand."

"But I thought you didn't want control of the company."

"I don't. But I do still own five percent of Preston stock and have a vested interest in ensuring the company thrives. It's not personal. It's just business."

"It's not business, it's treason. People are dying because of what you're doing. What about your country?"

"Oh, grow up, Claire. Didn't you learn anything in business school? Countries are nothing but remnants of a bygone age. It's a global economy. Corporations are all that matter, and this is good business. I'm simply making an investment in the future of this company."

"There is a difference between being a businessperson providing a necessary service and a profiteer getting rich off the blood of others."

The look he gave her couldn't have been more patronizing. "No, Claire. There really isn't."

She could only gape at him in horror. "You're out of your mind."

"Well, I suppose you would know."

Thinking Josh had said something along the same lines had wounded her to the core. Hearing it from Thad didn't faze her in the least. He was right. She did know what insanity looked like. She remembered how her mother had looked when her mind was gone; she knew the look she'd always feared she would one day find staring back at her in the mirror. That wasn't what she now saw burning in his eyes. What she saw staring back at her was madness all right, but a far more evil kind.

Pure, unadulterated greed.

Josh had accused her of feeling too much responsibility for the company. Maybe he was right. But it was far preferable to what she found herself facing now. Thad had never felt responsible for anyone other than himself, and this was the result.

"How did you even get involved with these people?"

"It was remarkably easy. I went down to human resources and got a list of all the recent applicants who'd failed their security checks. An instant list of possible terrorists. All it took was narrowing it down to one who actually had the right contacts."

"Ahmed Al-Saeed applied for a job here?"

"No, someone quite a bit further down the chain did. But that person got me an in that eventually led to Al-Saeed."

"And what? You offered them all this money and they took it, no questions asked?"

"No, they asked questions. To be honest, I wasn't sure

I was going to get out of there alive. The amusing thing is, I managed to convince them I support their cause. They think I'm casting off the shackles of my decadent American upbringing and the capitalist system that birthed me. Death to America, blah, blah, blah."

She could barely see through the fury blurring her vision. "Tell me, Thad. How many people have to die so that you can buy yourself a new Porsche?"

"Actually, I'm looking at an Aston Martin at the moment. And I have no idea." Nor, it was apparent, did he care.

"I'm not the only one who knows, you know. The government is investigating."

"Yes, I do know. They can investigate as much as they want. I admit I was a little sloppy covering my tracks at first, but I've remedied that situation. And with Father in charge rather than you or Milton, he'll need me to help out, and he need not have any idea what I'm doing under his nose."

The mention of Milton Vaughn brought back everything else Thad had to be responsible for. "You killed Milton."

"Ah, I promised you the truth about that, didn't I? As a matter of fact, yes, I did. Milton heard the rumors from some of his government cronies and was starting to look into them, which meant he had to be taken care of."

"But why frame me for it?"

"You have no one to blame for that but yourself."

"Me?"

"Yes. You wanted a closer look at the accounts from all the divisions. I couldn't have you looking at the books, because, like Milton, you might have noticed the money I borrowed to fund my business partners."

"And when he gave me access is when you started drugging me."

"You really have figured it all out, haven't you?" he said with feigned admiration. "I needed a way to distract you both. Having you wig out certainly did the trick. He stopped looking into the terrorist connection and you stopped looking at the books as you both wondered if you were losing it."

"So why bother killing him?"

"Because it couldn't go on forever. Eventually, Milton might be forced to conclude you were mentally unfit to take over, and the company would be sold. Or you might actually go to a doctor and find out what was really wrong with you."

"Instead, you killed Milton, set it up to look like I did, and left Gerald to find the scene."

"And I just happened to have dropped by the office to pick something up. When he told me how you must have lost your mind, I said I'd heard of a place we could get you quietly admitted for the right price, and everything unfolded exactly as planned. Actually, none of this would have worked if all of you weren't so thoroughly predictable. You each did exactly what I knew you would."

"Like my escape from Thornwood?"

The first trace of anger disturbed his smug expression. "No, that was unexpected. Which brings us to the loose end I mentioned needed tying."

He cocked the gun, the sound so loud in the stillness it might as well have been a shot. And smiled.

"Go ahead and scream. No one will hear you."

He was right. They were far enough from the party that no one was anywhere nearby.

The vast emptiness of the room seemed to stretch out endlessly around her, emphasizing how isolated she was.

This was what she'd wanted. To be on her own two feet. On her own. Alone.

And she *was* alone. The burst of realization was so potent it nearly rocked her back on her heels. Not just at this moment, but entirely. She'd never felt it as keenly as she did now, staring down the barrel of Thad's gun.

All those people she'd tried to show, to impress, by doing it on her own. Would any of them care if she died? Would anybody at all? Her father was dead. She'd never let anyone close, let anyone care. She had the painful feeling that now no one would.

And she wanted that, perhaps even more than to save her own life. Someone. Not someone in front of her, protecting her. Not someone behind her, ready to catch her if she fell. But someone beside her, just to be there with her, as she fought her own battles. Someone to care.

Josh had been that someone for the last three days, someone she'd never had before.

She wanted that. She wanted someone.

No, not just someone.

She wanted Josh.

But if she was to have any hope of seeing him again, she had to save herself first.

JOSH QUICKLY SCANNED the crowd for any sign of Claire or Thad. He saw none. Despite his desperate hope, they hadn't slipped back into the crowd.

He shifted his focus. There were five doors lining the wall closest to where he'd last seen Claire. The one he'd used to enter the party led to the kitchen. That still left four.

There was a uniformed security guard standing by one of the remaining doors. Josh quickly made his way to the man. He was tall, fifty-something, balding with a paunch. His name tag read Myers.

"Excuse me." Josh tried to keep his fear from showing, not wanting to make the guard wary. It was damn near impossible with the blood pumping through his veins. How the hell had Claire managed to do it?

"Can I help you?"

"Yes. Has a woman come through here? Brown hair, dark blue dress. She might have been with a tall, dark-haired man."

"Is there a problem, sir?" Josh must not have hidden his edginess well. A thread of suspicion ran through the guard's deferential tone.

Josh struggled to control his voice when all he wanted to do was throw the man back against the wall and demand an answer to his question. "I'm a friend of hers. I have reason to believe she may be in danger."

The guard's eyes widened. "Miss Claire? She was with Mr. Preston."

"Thad Preston?" Myers nodded. "Hell. Which way did they go?"

"Right through—"

Josh was off and moving as soon as the guard motioned to a door, not letting him complete the comment.

He burst into a long corridor that seemed to go on forever. It was empty. He took off, hesitating at every door he passed, listening for voices.

Before he knew it, there was someone behind him. He glanced back. Myers. "What's going on?"

Josh kept moving, pushing doors open, checking every open one. "Claire's in trouble. I don't have time to explain."

Breathing heavily, the guard followed on his heels, his

weight slowing him down. "Sir, if something's wrong, maybe I should alert the rest of the security staff on duty," he said warily, distrust in every word.

"Do it," Josh shot back. "Someone has to find her. *Now.*"

His vehemence seemed to have gotten to the guard. Josh heard him fumbling for his radio.

Josh didn't stick around. He took off, glancing in every room he passed, having no idea where he was going, only knowing he had to find her, had to know she was safe.

Even when every instinct he possessed was screaming that she wasn't.

QUICKLY TRYING TO COME UP with a plan, Claire slowly backed away from Thad. "You can't seriously believe you'll get away with this."

"Of course I will."

"By shooting me? You don't think anyone will figure that out?"

"It's not the preferred option, but I'm sure I can fake a suicide if necessary. Poor driven, workaholic Claire, knowing you're unfit to take over, doing the right thing by handing the reins to Gerald, but unable to deal with actually seeing it happen. So you retreat to a quiet spot and end it all. It could work."

"It's absurd."

"Maybe, but do you really think anyone would question it? It's too bad you moved when you did. A quick blow to the back of the head, and everything would have finished exactly as I planned, with you dying in a tragic accident just after your birthday. Maybe it still will."

She had no trouble connecting the dots. "That was why they started having me sit in the sun over the last few weeks at Thornwood. You were going to take me out of there and arrange for me to have an 'accident.'"

"Naturally. You've been in sunny Hawaii. I couldn't have you looking like you'd been sitting in a rubber room for four months." He shook his head. "Poor Claire. Comes all the way to attend Gerald's party only to drown in the reflecting pool. Mother and Father actually thought I was going to find a double to pretend to be you and sign the papers ceding control of the company to him. Which seems like a huge hassle when having you turn up dead will accomplish the same thing."

"But Gerald wouldn't inherit control of the company upon my death. My will doesn't stipulate to that."

"After everything I've managed to pull off, do you really think I'd have any trouble making a will disappear? Anything is possible if you have enough money. And we are your only living relatives. Or perhaps I'll make things easier and come up with a convincing new will superceding your old one and leaving everything to Father."

"Too bad it's not going to work."

Desperation darkened his face. "Yes, it will. I have worked too hard."

"People saw me leave the party with you. They'll know you did it."

"They might suspect, but they'll have no way to prove it. Besides, I don't have a motive, remember? I don't want control of the company."

Josh's warning words came back to her. He'd been referring to Gerald, but the statement applied just as well to Thad. He was long past the point of thinking rationally. He was desperate enough to do anything.

As though conjured from her mind, she heard his voice.

"Claire!"

She jerked her gaze toward the doorway behind Thad. She hadn't imagined it. That really was Josh. He was here.

His name automatically leaped into her throat to call out. It never reached her lips. Because if she called, he would come.

And Thad would shoot him.

Even now, she watched Thad's eyes shift nervously from her to the door and back again.

"Claire!" he called again. Closer this time.

Her heart thudded painfully in her chest. She had to warn him. She had to tell him to stay away.

The gun moved away from her. The action only renewed her terror.

She didn't even think. She simply reacted.

She jumped for the arm holding the gun, clamping down on his wrist. Thad immediately tried to shake her off.

He almost didn't manage it. Then, at the last second, her damned heel slipped on the slick floor, sending her foot flying out from under her. She felt it happen in slow motion, each movement stretched out to an eternity. Trying to retain her balance on the other wobbly heel. Throwing her arms out to even herself. The split second when it seemed she might make it. The split second when the heel finally gave way. Then she was falling, falling endlessly through the air.

She landed flat on her back with a painful thud, all the wind forced from her lungs by the blow.

She didn't even have time to react to having the air knocked out of her. Before she could blink, Thad's face appeared right over hers. She felt his fingers grab a fistful of hair at the top of her head and pull hard. Pain ripped through her scalp as he lifted her head and slammed it back against the ground. The first blow blurred her vision. Stars exploded before her eyes.

The second blow left her incapable of feeling any pain at all, stealing her eyesight and all conscious thought.

And as the darkness closed in, her last thought wasn't for her own safety, but for Josh's. She couldn't let anything happen to him.

She opened her mouth to offer some kind of warning. Nothing came out. It was too late.

THE SCENE BEFORE HIM brought Josh to an abrupt halt as soon as he entered the atrium. Shock immobilized his limbs.

Claire was prone on the ground, Thad poised over her, rolling her over and over toward a reflecting pool in the center of the room.

Oh, God. Was he too late? Was she dead?

Shaking off his stupor, Josh lurched forward just as Thad pushed Claire to the edge of the pool.

Noticing his presence, Thad quickly jerked to his feet, simultaneously lifting the gun he grasped in one hand and aiming it squarely at Josh's chest. "Stay right there."

This time it took every ounce of power he possessed to stop moving. He somehow managed it, stumbling to a stop.

His eyes shot to Claire. For a split second, Josh caught the slight rise and fall of her chest. She was alive.

He didn't have time to feel a moment's relief. In the next breath, Thad kicked Claire with his foot, sending her tumbling into the pool.

She landed in the water with a splash.

Face down.

She didn't move, clearly unconscious.

She could drown in a foot of water.

"Well, that was convenient," Thad said. "Your appearance, on the other hand, is not."

The hand holding the gun shook the slightest bit. His finger tensed on the trigger.

Josh fought against every instinct that wanted to rush to Claire and pull her out of the water. Thad would shoot him before he got halfway there, and then he wouldn't be able to do anything for her. No, he had to stay calm, had to figure out a way to get past Thad without getting himself too hurt to help her.

Even as Claire floated there, drowning before his very eyes.

He stepped forward, his hands held up at his side, trying not to spook the man with any sudden movements. "It's over, Thad. We both know it. You might be able to convince people that Claire died an accidental death, but not if you shoot me."

"Don't be so sure. I can be very persuasive when I have to be."

The words contained all the confidence his body language didn't. A frantic gleam shone in his eyes. Beads of sweat dotted his brow. Josh could practically see the thoughts racing through his head. At any second Thad could pull the trigger.

"Besides," he continued, a frenzied note entering his voice. "Maybe Claire shot you. After all, she's the crazy one. And then she fell. Yes, that makes sense—"

Another set of footsteps coming closer echoed from the entryway. Josh had forgotten about Myers on his heels. Thad's attention shifted away from Josh for the slightest of moments.

It was all Josh needed. He leaped toward the man, diving

for his torso. Thad didn't have time to lower his arm before Josh tackled him. They crashed to the ground. In the back of his mind, Josh registered the clatter of something else tumbling across the floor and knew Thad must have lost hold of the gun. Pushing himself up on one fist, he sent the other crashing into the man's face. No doubt dazed from falling with Josh on top of him, Thad didn't even react before the fist struck him in the jaw. His eyes rolled up, his head falling back onto the cement with a thud.

Josh would have loved nothing more than to keep on hitting him. But Claire was still in danger. He shoved to his feet, already stumbling toward the pool.

"What the—"

Myers. "Call 911!" Josh shouted. He didn't look to see if the guard did it. He reached the water's edge and launched himself into the pool, thrashing through the waves that dragged at his legs to get to her. With what seemed like unbearable slowness, he finally reached her and gently turned her over. Her eyes were still closed, her lips faintly blue. She wasn't breathing anymore. His heart stopped dead in his chest for a moment, but he didn't let himself stop. He dragged her to the side and pulled her out of the pool.

He immediately began CPR, his body going through the movements he knew by rote, his mind screaming with fear. Desperation seized his chest, suffocating him even as he tried to return the breath to her lungs.

"Come on, Claire. Come back to me."

He heard the words over and over again. He didn't know if he was saying them or they were simply a mantra repeating in his head.

A face filled his mind, blinding him to all else. Someone he was fighting for. Someone he had to save.

But the face he saw wasn't his mother's. It wasn't Maggie Flynn's or any of the other patients he'd ever lost.

There was only this woman, the woman he'd just found, the woman he loved.

He couldn't lose her. Not now. Not like this.

Terror unlike anything he'd ever known gripped him, and he was besieged with the feeling that he was fighting not just for her life, but for his own.

She coughed.

He froze, so shocked by the sound he wasn't sure at first he hadn't imagined it.

She did it again. A torrent of water burst from her mouth.

Relief slammed through him, damn near knocking the breath from his lungs, as the sound was followed quickly by another.

He'd never heard anything sweeter.

He discontinued compressions, reaching up as she slowly turned her head and spit up more water.

She blinked rapidly, her eyes shifting around as though trying to figure out where she was. They finally connected with his, widening. Something that looked suspiciously like tears shimmered in them.

"You're okay," she whispered, her voice clogged with emotion.

Nothing she said could have surprised him more. "Me? You're the one who took an unexpected swim."

Her eyes clouded in confusion for a split second, as though she was just registering her drenched state and the water she'd just coughed up. Then her forehead cleared. "You saved me."

"Yeah," he admitted. "Sorry about that."

There was no anger or bitterness in her eyes. "Thank you," she whispered.

"Believe me, I was just returning the favor."

A ghost of a smile touched her lips.

Then she frowned, alarm in her eyes as she jerked her head to look around her surroundings. "Thad?"

"Easy. You shouldn't move." Josh glanced back to where the man was still slumped on the floor. "He's down for the count. Don't worry. He's not going to get away with this, or anything else. We'll prove everything he's done."

"My purse. Did he throw my purse in the pool?"

Josh looked around until he spotted her bag sitting a few feet away. "No. It's right over there."

"Get it."

The urgency in the order surprised him. Not about to deny her anything in her present condition, he reached over and grabbed the bag.

"Open it," she ordered when she saw he had it.

He did as instructed. Other than her billfold and a tube of lipstick, there was only one other object inside. He pulled it out.

A microcassette recorder.

The buttons to activate its record function were depressed. Looking closer, he saw the spokes turning the tape continued to revolve. It was still recording.

"After what the agents said, I wanted to try to get a confession," Claire explained. "It just ended up coming from someone different than who I expected."

She grinned, and he had to do the same. Even pale, soaked and disheveled, she was beautiful.

"Proving everything should be a lot easier with that, don't you think?"

Epilogue

"Turkey and Swiss with mustard."

With a grin, Claire accepted the sandwich Josh offered her. "Just how I like it."

"I aim to please." He grinned back at her and reached into the bag for his own lunch.

Contentment swelled in her chest. She could have watched him all day. After a month she still couldn't get enough of him. Every time she looked at him her pulse kicked up several notches. Every time he was near she felt that now familiar hum.

Unwrapping her sandwich, Claire gazed out across the park. It was a beautiful afternoon. A gentle breeze rippled the grass. Children ran about on the green lawns. A few people played with their dogs. She took a deep breath and soaked in the peacefulness of the scene.

It had been a month since Gerald's ill-fated party. He'd never managed to make his announcement after all. From what she'd heard afterward, he'd just taken the podium when the arrival of the police and paramedics had distracted the crowd, not letting him get a word out. And then Thad had been arrested, and all hell had broken loose.

In the aftermath, Gerald had quietly stepped down from his position at the company. Claire hadn't heard a word from him or Dinah, not a single apology for their actions in the wake of Milton's death or what their son had done. When she was feeling generous, she supposed they had enough on their hands dealing with Thad's pending federal charges, not to mention their own criminal charges.

Mostly, though, she was too busy, trying to clean up the mess their son had left her, to worry about them. It wasn't going to be easy. She had federal investigators poring over every inch of the company, and the majority of the company's government contracts had been canceled or suspended. But she wasn't about to let her employees lose their jobs and her grandfather's and father's legacy—her legacy—be destroyed without a fight because of what Thad had done.

And through it all, she had Josh. They were both busy, since he was now back at work at the hospital. But they'd made a commitment to make time for each other, like their regular lunch date. And with each passing day, her love for this man only grew.

Thornwood had been closed. It seemed the rest of the patients there were legitimately in need of psychiatric care, but mistreatment was found to be rampant throughout. A cursory investigation of the staff had revealed that many, like Hobbs, had criminal records, which was how Emmons had been able to hire them for cheap, keeping his costs down and the money flowing to his gambling addiction. The other patients had been moved to other, no doubt better, facilities.

"Do you need anything else?" Josh asked, breaking into her thoughts.

"Nope," she said happily. "I have everything I need."

They were about to dig in when the clatter of plastic against the ground drew their attention downward. A Frisbee had landed at their feet.

"Hey, a little help!"

They looked up to see a boy, no more than eight, waving his hands a short distance away. Behind him, other children stood expectantly, no doubt the ones he'd been throwing the Frisbee with.

Josh reached down, picked up the disc, and sent it flying back to the boy with an expert flick of his wrist.

"Thanks!" the boy called back, leaping to catch the disc in midair. He'd barely hit the ground before he was off and running to rejoin his friends, tossing the Frisbee to one of his playmates along the way. Excited shouts and chatter filled the air.

As they finished their lunch, Claire noticed how Josh's attention would occasionally drift back to the kids, a gentle smile curving his lips. Something about the way he looked after them inspired an unexpected pang in her chest. And she realized she had one secret left.

She took a breath, suddenly nervous even though she didn't think she really had reason to be. "There's something I need to tell you," she said hesitantly, regaining his attention. "It may be premature, because we haven't even talked about the future, and I'm guessing it may not even be an issue. But I don't want there to be any secrets between us."

He frowned with concern. "What is it?"

"I decided a long time ago that I can never have biological children. I don't know for certain that whatever mental illness afflicted my family in the past is truly hereditary, or if it is, whether there's a chance I would pass it on. Regardless, it's a risk I can't take. I never want to force a child to have to deal with the same uncertainty and fear and painful scrutiny that I did. So when I was twenty-two I had a procedure to ensure it won't happen. I will never give birth to children of my own, so if you want biological children, I can't give them to you. I know that's an issue for some men, so I thought you should know before we go any further."

The warmth in his eyes eased her nervousness before he said a single word. "You're right. It's not an issue, but I appreciate you telling me. If and when we do decide to have children, there are other ways to do so. That is, if you even want kids."

She'd never really thought about it beyond ensuring she would never have her own. But she knew he would be a good father, and the idea of raising children with him suddenly seemed infinitely appealing. "Maybe. Someday."

"Well, if not, I can continue to help as many kids as possible in other ways, even if they're not mine. And if parenthood is something we ever decide to pursue, there are plenty of kids out there in need of a good home."

Kids like the boy he'd once been, she thought with a lump in her throat. Kids who needed to know they were safe and loved and wanted.

She reached up and touched his cheek. "And they'll know they only have to smile when they feel like it."

At that, he did smile, a big, beautiful, open smile that left no doubt to its authenticity. The sight of it filled her with such a sense of lightness and joy that she had to smile, too.

Then he did something that knocked the breath clear out of her lungs.

He said, "I love you."

She actually felt her heart stop. It was the first time

either of them had said it. She hadn't expected him to do so, hadn't even realized how much she'd wanted him to until this moment.

Three words. She'd never known three little words could mean so much, or feel so right.

"I love you, too," she whispered, even if those words didn't begin to express what she felt for this man.

It didn't matter. They were enough. They felt right.

He reached over and pulled her into his arms. Her heart began to pound wildly, unevenly. She made no attempt to try to control it. Because for perhaps the first time in her life she didn't have a doubt in the world.

This moment was real. This man and everything she felt for him, and he for her, were completely true.

And good for a lifetime.

* * * * *

Her breath whistled out in a sigh of relief when he exited Customs. Devon recognized him right away from the newspaper and magazine articles her friend and partner Sabrina had looked up during her frantic prep work.

Caleb John Logan, Jr. Thirty-one. Six-two. With jet-black hair, laser-blue eyes and a linebacker's shoulders under his charcoal-gray cashmere overcoat. His jaw-dropping good looks didn't score him any points with Devon. She'd learned the hard way not to trust handsome heartbreakers like Cal Logan.

But he was a client. An important one. And she was willing to give someone who'd served a hitch in the marines before earning a B.S. from the University of Oregon, an MBA from Stanford and his first million at the ripe old age of twenty-six the benefit of the doubt.

Right up until he spotted the hot-pink pashmina, that is.

Devon knew the flash of color was more visible than the sign she held up with his name on it. So she wasn't surprised when Logan picked her out of the crowd and cut in her direction. She'd just plastered on her best businesswoman smile when he whipped an arm around her waist. The next moment she was sprawled against his cashmere-covered chest.

"Hello, brown eyes."

Swooping down, he covered her mouth with his.

Sheer astonishment kept Devon rooted to the spot for a few seconds while her mind whirled chaotically. Her first thought was that her client had downed a few too many drinks during the long flight. Her second, that he'd mistaken the kind of escort and consulting services her company provided. Her third shoved everything else out of her head.

The man could kiss!

His mouth moved over hers with a skill that ignited sparks at a half dozen flash points throughout her body. Devon hadn't experienced that kind of spontaneous combustion in a while. A *long* while.

The sparks were still popping when she pushed off his chest, only now they fueled a flush of anger.

"Do you always greet women you don't know with a lip-lock, Mr. Logan?"

A smile crinkled the skin at the corners of his eyes. "As a matter of fact, I don't. That was from Don."

"Huh?"

"He said he owed you one from New Year's Eve two years ago and made me promise to deliver it."

She stared up at him in total incomprehension. Logan hooked a brow and attempted to prompt a nonexistent memory.

"He abandoned you at the Waldorf. Five minutes before midnight. To deliver twins."

"I don't have a clue who or what you're..."

Understanding burst like a water balloon.

"Wait a sec. Are you talking about Sabrina's old boyfriend? Your buddy, who's now an ob-gyn doc?"

It was Logan's turn to look startled. He recovered faster than Devon had, though. His smile widened into a rueful grin.

"I take it you're not Sabrina Russo."

"No, Mr. Logan, I am *not*."

* * * * *

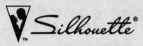

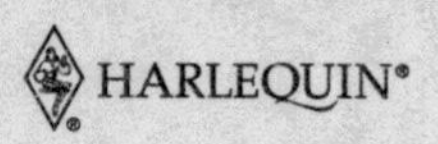

INTRIGUE®

COMING NEXT MONTH

#1095 CHRISTMAS AWAKENING by Ann Voss Peterson
A Holiday Mystery at Jenkins Cove
The ghost of Christmas present looms over Brandon Drake when his butler's daughter returns to Drake House. Can Marie Leonard and the scarred millionaire find answers in their shared past that will enable them to catch her father's killer?

#1096 MIRACLE AT COLTS RUN CROSS by Joanna Wayne
Four Brothers of Colts Run Cross
When their twins are kidnapped, Nick Ridgely and Becky Collingsworth face the biggest crisis in their marriage yet. Will the race to save their children bring them closer in time for an old-fashioned Texas Christmas?

#1097 SILENT NIGHT SANCTUARY by Rita Herron
Guardian Angel Investigations
When Leah Holden's seven-year-old sister goes missing, she turns to detective Kyle McKinney. To reunite this family, Kyle will do anything to find the child, even if it means crossing the line with the law...and with Leah.

#1098 CHRISTMAS CONFESSIONS by Kathleen Long
Hunted by a killer who's never been caught, Abby Conroy's world is sent into a tailspin, which only police detective Gage McDermont can pull her out of. One thing is certain: this holiday season's going to be murder…

#1099 KANSAS CITY CHRISTMAS by Julie Miller
The Precinct: Brotherhood of the Badge
Edward Kincaid has no reason to celebrate Christmas—until he begins playing reluctant bodyguard to Dr. Holly Robinson. Now, the M.E. who can bust the city's biggest case wide open might also be the only one able to crack Edward's tough shell.

#1100 NICK OF TIME by Elle James
Santa's missing from the North Pole and his daughter, Mary Christmas, can't save the holiday by herself. It's up to cowboy and danger-junkie Nick St. Clair to find the jolly ol' fellow in time for the holidays, before Christmas is done for as he knows it…